"For what it's worth, I'm not such a bad guy."

True enough, Chloe agreed, but there must be a reason Jake Braddock hadn't gotten full custody of Brianna.

"You don't believe me?" Jake asked.

"Sure I do." She tried to force sincerity into her smile, yet a veil of skepticism slid over his angular face. He didn't object, which she appreciated. She wasn't up for a confrontation until after she'd had her morning coffee.

She decided to flirt and make him squirm a little, but she'd have to put that on hold and take care of her morning caffeine addiction. Though her craving for a hot cup of java was calling her, she glanced over her shoulder to find Jake's eyes locked on her.

A grin tugged at her lips as she returned to her quest for coffee. Jake Braddock was her favorite type of challenge.

And he'd ju

D0834689

Dear Reader,

Can you believe it's June already?

It's time for barbecues, picnics and fun in the sun. I don't know about you, but during the lazy days of summer, I take a book to the pool or the beach and escape for an afternoon. And I hope that's what you'll do with *The Cowboy's Lullaby*.

For those of you who have been fans of THE BAYSIDE BACHELORS series, this is another for your collection. Only this story isn't about a one-time delinquent who made good. Instead, it's about Chloe Haskell, Joe Davenport's sexy, kindhearted neighbor. Chloe is far more heroic and loveable than people give her credit for being. Still, she has a journey to make that will earn her the right to have her own happily ever after.

I hope you enjoy reading *The Cowboy's Lullaby* as much as I enjoyed writing it.

Wishing you romance,

Judy

THE COWBOY'S LULLABY

JUDY DUARTE

Silhouette

SPECIAL EDITION®

Published by Silhouette Books

America's Publisher of Contemporary Romance

If you purchased this book without a cover you should be aware that this book is stolen property. It was reported as "unsold and destroyed" to the publisher, and neither the author nor the publisher has received any payment for this "stripped book."

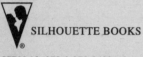

SILHOUETTE BOOKS

ISBN-13: 978-0-373-24834-6
ISBN-10:   0-373-24834-2

THE COWBOY'S LULLABY

Copyright © 2007 by Judy Duarte

All rights reserved. Except for use in any review, the reproduction or utilization of this work in whole or in part in any form by any electronic, mechanical or other means, now known or hereafter invented, including xerography, photocopying and recording, or in any information storage or retrieval system, is forbidden without the written permission of the editorial office, Silhouette Books, 233 Broadway, New York, NY 10279 U.S.A.

This is a work of fiction. Names, characters, places and incidents are either the product of the author's imagination or are used fictitiously, and any resemblance to actual persons, living or dead, business establishments, events or locales is entirely coincidental.

This edition published by arrangement with Harlequin Books S.A.

® and TM are trademarks of Harlequin Books S.A., used under license. Trademarks indicated with ® are registered in the United States Patent and Trademark Office, the Canadian Trade Marks Office and in other countries.

Visit Silhouette Books at www.eHarlequin.com

Printed in U.S.A.

Books by Judy Duarte

Silhouette Special Edition

Cowboy Courage #1458
Family Practice #1511
Almost Perfect #1540
Big Sky Baby #1563
The Virgin's Makeover #1593
Bluegrass Baby #1598
The Rich Man's Son #1634
**Hailey's Hero* #1659
*Their Secret Son #1667
**Their Unexpected Family* #1676
Worth Fighting For #1684

The Matchmakers' Daddy #1689
His Mother's Wedding #1731
Call Me Cowboy #1743
†*The Perfect Wife* #1773
Rock-A-Bye Rancher #1784
Daddy on Call #1822
The Cowboy's Lullaby #1834

*Bayside Bachelors
**Montana Mavericks
†Talk of the Neighborhood

Silhouette Books

**Double Destiny
 "Second Chance"

JUDY DUARTE

always knew there was a book inside her, but since English was her least favorite subject in school, she never considered herself a writer. An avid reader who enjoys a happy ending, Judy couldn't shake the dream of creating a book of her own.

Her dream became a reality in March of 2002, when the Silhouette Special Edition line released her first book, *Cowboy Courage*. Since then, she has sold nineteen more novels.

Her stories have touched the hearts of readers around the world. And in July of 2005, Judy won a prestigious Reader's Choice Award for *The Rich Man's Son*.

Judy makes her home near the beach in Southern California. When she's not cooped up in her writing cave, she's spending time with her somewhat enormous, but delightfully close family.

You can write to Judy c/o Silhouette Books, 233 Broadway, Suite 1001, New York, NY 10237. You can also contact her at: JudyDuarte@sbcglobal.net or through her Web site www.judyduarte.com.

To Bob and Betty Astleford.
I couldn't have handpicked better parents.
I love you, Mom and Dad.

Chapter One

Jake Braddock was nursing a Monday-morning hangover and brewing a pot of coffee when the call came in, telling him that his stepmother, Desiree, had passed away.

"What do you mean she passed away?" he asked the hospital spokeswoman. Desiree hadn't even reached her fortieth birthday. "What happened?"

"Officially the cause of death was pneumonia. But it was cancer related."

Cancer?

Jake pulled out the black-and-chrome bar stool nearest to the phone line and took a seat, raking a hand through his hair. He cursed the throbbing in his head, which was now pounding like a son of a gun.

"I didn't know she was sick," he muttered. Not really. Well, not *that* sick.

A week or so ago, when she'd returned from San Diego for the last time, Jake had taken a good hard look at her and noticed dark circles under her eyes and a wan complexion. When he'd suggested she see a doctor, she'd said not to worry, that she was under medical care.

He'd suspected she was ill, but he hadn't had any idea that her condition was terminal.

"I, uh…" He stumbled over an explanation. "She and I…weren't very close."

Apparently not, the silence seemed to say.

He cleared his throat, hoping to clear his head, as well. "Let's start over. I knew she was sick, but she never mentioned cancer."

Or told him that she was dying.

"I'm sorry for your loss," the woman said. "Mrs. Braddock made all of her arrangements, so there isn't anything for you to do. I'm just following hospital protocol by notifying the next of kin."

"Then, I guess, that's me."

"And Chloe Haskell in San Diego."

Jake stiffened. "Who the hell is Chloe Haskell?"

"I don't know, sir. Mrs. Braddock listed the two of you as her next of kin."

"What about her daughter?" he asked.

"Would that be Ms. Haskell?"

"No, it wouldn't." Well, hell. Maybe it was. He supposed Desiree could have another child. Older, maybe. Grown. Like him. He hadn't really known his stepmother that well, other than the fact she'd been a topless dancer before marrying his old man.

Either way, now he'd have to tell Brianna, his nearly five-year-old half sister, that her mommy had died. Of course, he'd have to find her first. Desiree had been traveling back and forth to San Diego for the past couple of months, but last week she'd returned to Dallas without the child.

And that was odd.

Jake might have issues with Desiree about a lot of things, but he'd come to realize she was a devoted mother. At least, that had been his opinion before she'd left Brianna in San Diego.

When he'd questioned her about it, she'd said, "Brianna is staying with a dear friend. She's happy and well cared for."

Jake didn't know much about his stepmother's friends, although he suspected they all worked at the same San Diego strip club Desiree used to manage, so he had good reason to feel uneasy.

Maybe Brianna was with Chloe—whoever she was.

"There's no one else on my contact list," the spokeswoman said. "Just you and Miss Haskell, whom I've already called."

The hospital had notified someone other than Jake *first?*

He cursed, although he wasn't sure whether it was at the news he'd just heard or the hammering in his head and the bile swirling in his gut.

"I'm sorry," the woman on the line said. "Is there someone I can call for you? Perhaps a grief counselor from hospice?"

"No. This is just a…" He was going to say it was a shock, but he bit back the rest of his sentence. Desiree was his stepmother, and she lived…well, she *used* to live just an hour or so away from him. Her death and the fact that she'd been suffering from cancer for God-only-knew-how-long shouldn't have come as a surprise. Not if she'd kept him more in the loop.

Of course, once his sixty-year-old father met her on a cruise ship, Jake and his wishes had been bypassed entirely. Talk about a midlife crisis. His old man's had been a humdinger.

Gerald Braddock had always been conservative in everything he did, but he'd fallen head over heels for a former topless dancer, who was twenty-eight and young enough to be his daughter. And he'd married her faster than a spinning tassel on a pastie.

Okay, so his dad had seemed happier in the past six years than Jake had ever seen him before, but that was probably because of Brianna, the daughter he'd fathered with his new wife.

An only child, Jake had always wanted a brother or sister, but he hadn't planned on getting one when he was twenty-eight. Still, Brianna was a cutie and had quickly wrapped her big brother around her little finger.

Jake didn't see her as often as he would have liked for several reasons. For one thing, his business ventures kept him busy. And for another, he tried to avoid Desiree whenever he could.

Desiree broached him about it a couple of times, implying she wanted to be on friendlier terms, but even after he'd gotten over the shock of his father's second marriage, he just couldn't bring himself to accept his new stepmother as a part of the family.

"I'm sorry for your loss," the hospital spokeswoman added.

"Yeah. Thanks."

When the line disconnected, Jake continued to grip the receiver as though he could somehow gain control of everything that had slipped out of his hands—first his father's marriage and then his death.

And now this.

Jake had never liked Desiree. Of course, if truth be told, he'd never given her a chance, even though his father had repeatedly asked him to. But how could he when the young woman had married his old man for money?

The proof came when she hightailed it to an attorney to amend the trust the day after Gerald Braddock's funeral.

On Jake's part, the issue had little to do with greed. He'd been successful in his own right. He also held fifty-one percent of the stock in Braddock Enterprises, a Dallas company that oversaw various oil and petroleum-related business ventures. He didn't like to boast, but the value of each share had nearly doubled since he'd taken the helm.

So it wasn't the money he was after. Jake just didn't like the idea that his father had been hoodwinked by a woman who didn't fit into his social sphere. A woman who'd convinced him to spend more time at the ranch and less in the city, where he had a spacious, luxury home that was much closer to the office.

Of course, Desiree had absolutely no class when it came to high-society expectations, so it was no wonder his dad had gravitated toward the ranch and started playing cowboy, even though he was in his sixties.

He was also playing daddy, a small voice reminded him. *And doing a better job of it the second time around.*

Jake's thoughts immediately turned to Brianna, to the orphan who needed him to step up to the plate and play daddy now.

But he didn't know where to find her.

He could hire a P.I., but a call to Desiree's attorney might provide an immediate answer. He pulled out the phone book and thumbed through the pages until he found a number for Brian Willoughby, Esquire.

A receptionist answered and, when he told her why he'd called, she put him on hold.

Seconds later, the attorney came on the line. "Hello, Mr. Braddock. I've been expecting your call."

Yeah, well, it looked like everyone in the world knew about Desiree's cancer—everyone but Jake. And the whole sorry, rotten mess put him in a foul mood. Hell, he'd felt better when he'd only had a hangover to deal with.

"I was sorry to hear that Desiree passed away," Willoughby added.

He'd already heard? The pounding in Jake's head grew more insistent. "How did you find out about her death so soon?"

"Ms. Haskell called a few moments ago."

Jake had the urge to hurl the telephone receiver across the room. Who the hell *was* that woman?

"Fortunately," Willoughby said, "Desiree took utmost care in dealing with the legalities."

"That doesn't surprise me in the least." Jake figured she'd been itching to get her hands on the money and take control of the company the moment she stepped foot on that cruise ship and scoped out Gerald Braddock.

Damn. He still couldn't fathom the two of them together.

"Desiree was a courageous woman," Willoughby said. "And strong. I came to admire her a great deal."

"Well, since you seem to have such a clear understanding and appear to be more aware of what's going on than I am, tell me where I can find my sister."

"She's in San Diego with Ms. Haskell. And from what I understand, she's doing as well as can be expected."

"If you'd be so kind as to give me an address, I'll get a flight out today and pick her up."

"That won't be necessary."

Jake bristled. "What are you talking about?"

"Desiree has left temporary custody of Brianna to Ms. Haskell, at least until the will is read. However, there are a few stipulations and particulars I need to discuss with both of you at the reading regarding joint custody. And unfortunately, I'm not available until Friday morning. Ms. Haskell said that works for her. I hope it fits your schedule, too. Otherwise, we'll have to postpone our meeting until next week."

"I'd rather not put this off any longer than necessary." Jake was already reaching for his Blackberry, eager to call in his own attorney. No, make that an entire law firm. This was crap. And he would contest the will at the top of his legal lungs.

The fact that Desiree had expected people from two different states to share custody of a child ready to enter kindergarten suggested that her mental state had been fading toward the end. The legal dream team he was about to put together ought to have a heyday with that issue and use it to put a stop to all of this pretty damn quick.

Jake didn't have a problem sharing the estate with Brianna, but he wouldn't share control with anyone else—especially a friend of his stepmother.

"Do you have a telephone number or an address for that woman?" he asked.

"You mean Ms. Haskell?"

"Yeah." Jake grabbed a pen and scratched out 146 Tahiti Circle, Bayside, California. "I thought she was in San Diego."

"From what I understand, that's a suburb."

Then, when Willoughby recited her number, he jotted it down, even though he had no intention of calling.

He was going to fly to California as soon as possible. Brianna lost her father last year and her mother today. She needed to be with family, with someone who loved her.

And that someone was her big brother, Jake.

Chloe Haskell hadn't been to the park in nearly ten years and wished she'd come sooner.

There was something liberating about swinging back and forth like a child again, allowing the summer breeze to muss her hair. She supposed there were some who would criticize a grown woman for enjoying herself in a playground, but Chloe couldn't care less. She was doing this for Brianna—and for the woman who should have been swinging beside the child instead.

"Let's go all the way up to Heaven," Brianna said.

If only they could.

Desiree had been a wonderful mother, a devoted friend.

Brianna must miss her terribly.

Chloe missed her, too. She and Desiree had been more like sisters than friends, even though they hadn't seen each other as often as they should have.

In retrospect, Chloe wished that she had taken time for personal visits to Dallas, but in her defense, she'd been busy, first attending college, then opening her own business. So the two women had kept in contact via long phone calls and e-mails.

There wasn't much they hadn't discussed over the past six years. When Chloe had decided to lease the old five-and-dime store in downtown Bayside and put in a dance studio, she'd called Desiree for advice. And Desiree, who'd retired once she'd moved to Dallas, shared the joys of married life with the wonderful older man she adored.

Of course, she also confided in Chloe about the problems she'd faced as a stepmother to her husband's son, a "kid" who vowed never to accept her.

When Desiree was blessed with a daughter and at last had the family she'd been waiting for, Chloe had been thrilled for her and sent gifts regularly—little dresses and outfits she'd picked up, books, a toy or two.

It was hard not to envy Desiree's good fortune—until her luck took a nasty turn.

First her husband suffered a massive heart attack and died, then, a couple of months ago, she brought Brianna out to California for what Chloe and the child believed was a special visit, a vacation of sorts.

But the reunion had been bittersweet.

"I need to ask you a favor," Desiree had told Chloe, as little Brianna played in the colorful indoor playground at Burger Bob's.

"Anything." Chloe withdrew the straw of her chocolate shake and licked a dollop from the end. "You know that."

Desiree wrapped the remainder of her burger into

the bright yellow paper it had come in and pushed it aside. "I need you to take care of Brianna for me."

"Of course," Chloe'd said. "I'd love to babysit."

"I'm afraid it's more permanent than that."

A cold chill that had nothing to do with the shake crept over Chloe, and she'd sensed Desiree's explanation before she could utter the words.

Desiree tore at the edge of her napkin, then peered at Chloe with glistening eyes. "My cancer came back."

While Chloe was in high school, Desiree had been diagnosed with lung cancer. When she'd completed her medical treatment and was in remission, Chloe's father, who'd been first her employer and later a business associate, had sent her on an all-expenses-paid cruise to Alaska, where she met Gerald Braddock.

"And it's terminal," Desiree'd added.

The reality and the implication of the diagnosis slammed into Chloe, releasing a torrent of shock and grief. "You need to get a second opinion."

"I've seen three different doctors, hoping for another diagnosis and more options. But they all agree. There's nothing that can be done."

The silence threatened to draw them into an emotional whirlpool, and it was all Chloe could do to hang on and not let it carry her away. Not while Brianna played just a few feet away.

"It sucks," Desiree had said. "It really does. I've waited for years to have a child, and now I'm going to leave her. And miss watching her grow up. But if there's anyone in this world who will love and care for Brianna the way I would have done, it's you."

"I..." Chloe had been dumbstruck. Desiree was only thirty-four—ten years older than Chloe. "Of course I'll take Brianna. I'll love her like my own. But maybe there's something that can be done, something experimental. A promising new treatment. Perhaps one of the doctors in San Diego—"

"I'm afraid there isn't anything that can be done."

And she'd been right. In less than four weeks, Desiree had died.

The memory of that day faded as little Brianna drew Chloe back to the present.

"Too bad we can't go to Heaven," Brianna said. "Mommy loves chocolate. And so does Daddy. We could take them some of the brownies we made."

"From what I understand, they have all the dessert anyone could ever want in Heaven. But you're right. We have too many to eat all by ourselves. Maybe we can share them with someone else."

Under the circumstances, Brianna seemed to be taking her mother's death fairly well. Of course, Desiree had been preparing her for the past month. And then the two of them had shared a tearful, final good-bye more than a week ago.

Sacrificing her last days must have been tough for Desiree. But she hadn't wanted Brianna's memories to be tainted by a hospital setting or seeing her mother connected to tubes and wires. So she left the girl with Chloe more than a week ago, then went home to die.

There was a child psychologist in Dallas whom Desiree had been taking Brianna to see, and Chloe had every intention of following through on those appointments. The little girl seemed to be doing okay, but Chloe didn't want her have any problems down the road.

"Tell me again how you met my mommy," Brianna said.

Chloe had known better than to be entirely truthful, especially with a child. So she stretched things a bit. Softened them.

"My father owned a...dance place," Chloe said. "And your mommy came looking for a job. I was a little girl, like you, and I thought she was the most beautiful dancer I'd ever seen."

Why tell the child that Chloe's father owned a bar and strip club? Or that on the day Desiree had shown up, she'd been sporting a black eye, a swollen jaw and a split lip?

"And then," Brianna said, adding to the story she'd already heard several times, "when your daddy needed someone to watch you, she was the bestest babysitter in the whole, wide world."

"That she was."

Chloe's father, Ron Haskell, was a gambler at heart and had won a seedy bar and strip club in a poker game. During the early years, when Chloe hadn't been much older than Brianna, she spent a lot of time at the club, where the cocktail waitresses and dancers used to look after her. Desiree, who loved children, gladly babysat whenever Ron asked her. Before long, she and Chloe had developed a strong, loving bond.

Desiree, who'd had a lousy childhood and absolutely no family support, had learned to rely on her available resources—her beauty, her body and an ability to read her customers and alter her dances to fulfill their fantasies. Too bad it took her ages to hone the same ability when it came to reading her lovers and realizing she was a loser magnet when it came to romance.

All Desiree had really wanted was love and a family, yet, that dream had remained out of reach for years. But that didn't mean she wasn't successful in other ways.

Ron wasn't a businessman, yet Desiree was a natural. And soon, thanks to her advice and managerial skills, the club began to turn a decent profit.

Desiree also prodded Ron to invest in other properties. With her innate business savvy and refusal to allow him to gamble all the profit away, Ron died a wealthy man.

"And because my mommy was so pretty and smart," Brianna said, reciting her version of what Chloe had been asked to repeat several times already, "and because she was a good dancer, you're making a book about her."

"It's not exactly a book. It's more like a journal of memories that you can read when you get older." Chloe had titled it *Lessons from Desiree*, which might be a bit lame, but creating it was somehow helping her deal with the loss of her best friend.

"And I get to write in it, too," Brianna reminded her. "As soon as I go to school and learn how to spell."

"That's right, Breezy."

They pumped their feet, swinging in silence for a while, the wind blowing Chloe's long, curly hair and whipping a red strand across her cheek. It was probably a tangled mess right now, but she didn't care.

She shot a sideways glance at Brianna, and when their gazes met, the child grinned. "You sure are a good swinger, Chloe. Just like my mom."

"Your mom was a wonderful teacher."

Brianna nodded, then scanned the small playground and gasped. "Oh! I need to get off. Can you help me?"

"Sure." Chloe jumped from her seat, landing upright in the sand. She walked to the back of Brianna's swing and slowed it to a stop. "What do you want to do now? You're not ready to go back to the house, are you?"

"No. I want to play with Jenny and Penny. And they finally got off the teeter-totter and are climbing the slide. I want to do that, too." Once her feet touched the ground, the little blonde, who favored her mommy, ran across the sand to join the two new playmates she'd recently met.

When Chloe had been a child, she hadn't had many friends her own age, something she sorely missed, so it was nice to see Brianna socialize.

Gosh, it was just plain nice to have Brianna around.

Yes, they'd had—and would continue to have—moments of sadness and tears, but Chloe was determined to do everything in her power to ensure that Brianna grew up happy and loved.

Still, at times, Chloe feared she may have bitten off more than she could chew in the agreement she'd made with Desiree. But not when it came to motherhood, a new role she'd easily fallen into. Her reservations stemmed from staying in Texas for six weeks, as Desiree had asked her to, and facing the legalities and trouble she was bound to run into when she met Brianna's stepbrother.

And the day of reckoning was closing in on her.

On Friday morning she would meet Jake Braddock in Dallas at Brian Willoughby's office.

Years ago Desiree had taught Chloe to always put her best foot forward, especially when facing adversity. And that meant dressing to the nines, carefully applying makeup and holding her head up high. That particular piece of advice was in *Lessons from Desiree* and labeled #1: "Always look your best."

And on Friday morning, Chloe intended to do just that. She would walk right into that meeting and take the upper hand.

Still, a feeling of dread settled over her whenever she thought about it.

Thank goodness she had a few more days to prepare mentally for the confrontation, which she expected the meeting to be. She'd promised to abide by

Desiree's wishes and she would insist that Jake comply with them, too.

Spotting a shiny glimmer in the sand, she stooped and reached for it.

A quarter.

Her father always said finding coins was a sign of luck, so when she and Brianna headed to the market later this afternoon, she'd have to buy a lottery ticket.

Just at that moment, Brianna squealed from atop the slide. "Jake!"

Chloe turned to see the little blonde slide to the bottom, lickety-split, then scamper toward a tall, well-dressed man approaching the playground with a sexy, Texas swagger.

Uh-oh.

She'd never met Jake Braddock, but she'd been told he had a young, brash J. R. Ewing aura. And this particular dark-haired man, with his expensive Western wear, had a stance that boasted money and power.

She brushed the quarter against the black fabric of her shorts, then tucked it into her pocket. She'd thought she had a couple of days before their confrontation, but it looked as though her time had run out.

She just hoped her luck hadn't run out, as well.

Chapter Two

At the sound of Brianna's voice, Jake picked up his pace and strode toward his baby sister. "Hey, munchkin. I've missed you."

She hurried to meet him and lost a flip-flop in the sand. Faltering only a moment, she ran on without it.

When she reached him, he lifted her into his arms, catching a whiff of gumdrops. At least Ms. Haskell had kept her clean and shampooed.

"I didn't think I would see you until a lot more days," Brianna said, giving him a pint-sized hug that squeezed the heart right out of him.

"Yeah, well, I didn't want to wait." He brushed a kiss upon her cheek.

"You know what?" she asked. "Mommy went to see Daddy in Heaven."

"I heard," he whispered against her hair, his voice cracking with grief for her loss. "And I came to take you home with me."

"Are you taking Chloe, too?" she asked. "She said I'm going to live with her."

Over Jake's dead body. And he'd lined up a legal team to make sure that wouldn't happen.

"Hello, there," a sultry, female voice said.

Jake turned to face a tall, shapely redhead who reminded him of Julia Roberts in her *Pretty Woman* days.

A scattering of freckles across her nose gave her a girlish appeal. But as his gaze dropped to a yellow bikini top and a pair of black shorts, he realized there was nothing remotely childlike about her body.

Damn.

Without a conscious thought, he zeroed in on a pair of long legs that could wrap around a guy, making his hormones kick up a notch and his brains leave town—permanently.

Double damn.

"Mr. Braddock?" she asked, reminding him it was his turn to respond.

He cleared his throat. "Yes." And she had to be Ms. Haskell. Chloe. Desiree's "dear" friend.

For a man who prided himself in maintaining control, he was having trouble finding his words.

"I've heard about you," she said.

He expected her to continue with one of those standard remarks, something about it being a pleasure to finally meet him. But since she didn't utter anything more, he wasn't sure what she'd heard about him.

In his attempt to distance himself from his stepmother, he'd neglected to consider what Desiree might think of him, what she might confide in her friends.

Not that it really mattered, he supposed.

Chloe shifted her weight and placed a hand on a shapely hip. He tried to read her body language, but his gaze merely locked on an impish spark in those green eyes, the hint of a pair of dimples, the fullness of her lips.

"Since we have an appointment in Dallas on Friday," she said, "it's a bit of a surprise to see you in California."

"I realize that, but I wanted to see my sister. I think it's best if she has family near her right now."

"Chloe's my family, too," Brianna said. "Mommy told me. They're the same as sisters."

"Oh, yeah?" Jake responded, sensing the showdown to come and prepared for it.

Yet when he glanced at Brianna, at the smile she wore, he realized this wasn't the time or place for a confrontation. Maybe he'd better tread easy, make nice. Lay on the charm until he could take Brianna home, then let the attorneys fight it out.

Brianna tapped him on the shoulder. "Could you please put me down? I lost my shoe."

He placed her on the ground, and she half hopped, half walked to get her missing pink flip-flop.

His full attention returned to Chloe, even though her presence had been nearly overwhelming once she'd come on scene.

"I have temporary custody of Brianna," she said, "until we meet in Dallas."

"Okay. But you'll have to forgive me for being concerned about her. All of this came as quite a shock."

Chloe crossed her arms under her breasts, causing them to swell before his eyes.

Didn't she have some kind of cover-up to wear?

He fingered the collar of his crisp white shirt and adjusted the knot of his tie. According to the weather report, it wasn't supposed to be anywhere near as warm in Bayside as it had been in Dallas, but it seemed as though he'd brought the heat and humidity with him.

"Brianna is doing as well as can be expected," Chloe said. "Desiree tried hard to prepare her."

"How can you prepare a five-year-old for something like death?"

"It's difficult for anyone, I suppose." Her voice was soft, laced with something. Grief? Compassion?

Whether it was sincere or not, he couldn't say. "I'm sure you can understand why I wanted to come and check on her. And why I want to take her home."

"She *is* home."

Before he could object, Brianna ran back and grabbed one of each of their hands. "Are you going to spend the night with us? We're having brownies for dinner. Chloe and I made them all by ourselves."

"I, uh…" He glanced at Chloe, feeling as awkward as an adolescent on hormone overdrive.

"It would be nice if you stayed for dinner with us," she said. "But from what I understand, you're a very busy man. So maybe we ought to take a rain check. Brianna and I will be flying to Dallas on Thursday evening and will be staying for a while. You can spend some time with her then."

She'd welcomed him to dinner politely, then blew him off at the same time, making it clear that she wasn't going to allow him to take Brianna without him making a scene—something he wasn't about to do.

Not if it caused Brianna any unnecessary sadness. She'd had far too much already.

"Maybe we can go to Buckaroo Roundup for dinner on Friday night," he told the child.

She brightened. "That will be so fun. I like to ride the pony in the game room. Will you get me a bunch of tokens?"

"You bet." A grin tweaked his lips. Score one for the home team. He'd make up for lost time as soon as they got back on his turf. Maybe he'd have to throw in a visit to the toy store, too. There was a lot he needed to make right.

In his attempt to avoid Brianna's mother, he'd inadvertently steered clear of his little sister, too. And he regretted it. Especially now.

"You'll like Buckaroo Roundup, too," Brianna

told Chloe. "They have ponies and other rides in the back room."

His gaze locked on Chloe's, and he sensed a don't-underestimate-me vibe.

He wouldn't. But she'd better not underestimate him, either. If she messed with the bull, she'd have to watch for the horns.

It was out of character for him to step down from a fight, to fly all the way to California, then leave without taking Brianna with him. But he didn't want the little girl to sense the power struggle brewing. He'd just bide his time—until Friday.

So he tossed his adversary a what-the-hell grin. "I'll see you in a couple of days, then."

Jake might have lost this minor skirmish, but he was determined to win the war.

And win custody of his sister.

After all, Chloe shouldn't be looking after—*or influencing*—a little girl.

What kind of woman wore a bikini to the park and fed brownies to a child for dinner, anyway?

As he strode toward the rental car he'd parked near the entrance of the condominium complex, he fought the urge to take another look at his pretty opponent. She had an attractive face and a dynamite body, but he doubted she had one maternal bone in her.

He just hoped she didn't have much fight in her, either. He planned to put a stop to this foolish custody thing by the end of the week.

In spite of his determination to climb into his vehicle and not look back, curiosity won out, and he turned, only to find her eyes locked on him.

He tipped his head, acknowledging her. And in return, she lifted her hand and fluttered her fingers in a wave. Then she crossed her arms, causing her breasts to stretch the limits of that bikini top.

The summer breeze blew a corkscrew strand of red hair across her face and she swiped it away.

He couldn't deny that looking at her caused his hormones to pump or his blood to heat. Heck, she'd have that effect on any man, he supposed.

But Jake had learned to control his impulses.

His old man might have fallen gray-head-over-boot heels for a topless dancer, but Jake had more sense than that.

Still he had to tear his gaze away from her and force himself to head for his car.

On Friday, at a quarter to twelve, Chloe and Brianna sat at a table in the restaurant of the Dallas hotel in which they'd stayed last night, waiting for Mrs. Davies to arrive.

Barbara Davies was the housekeeper at the Braddock ranch and had been hired by Desiree's husband shortly before he passed away. Since Brianna would need a sitter while Chloe was at the attorney's office, Barbara was asked to meet them at the hotel.

Believing Brianna should be around people she was familiar with during this difficult time, Desiree had given the housekeeper a raise and secured her services through a three-year employment contract.

"Barbara comes across as stuffy and snooty," Desiree had said, "but she's good with Brianna. And she's loyal."

Chloe didn't care for snobs, but she would have to trust Desiree on this one.

"There she is." Brianna waved at a salt-and-pepper-haired matron in her late fifties.

The pleasantly plump woman smiled at the child and strode toward their table, waddling as she approached.

Chloe stood to introduce herself, but decided to wait until Barbara had addressed Brianna.

"Welcome back to Texas," the woman told the child. "I've missed you, honey. That big old house isn't the same without your smile."

"I missed you, too. Did you feed my fish while I was gone?"

"I most certainly did. And I cleaned their bowl again this morning." The woman turned to Chloe, her gaze assessing her in rapid fashion, her nose drifting upward in a self-righteous manner. Or had that only been Chloe's imagination?

Either way, she reminded herself of Desiree's acceptance of the woman and reached out her arm in greeting. "How do you do?"

Mrs. Davies took her hand in a firm grip. "Very well, thank you."

"You're a bit early," Chloe said.

"Mr. Braddock always insisted on punctuality, and fortunately, I pride myself on being timely."

"Well, good. Why don't you join us for lunch?"

"I had a late breakfast, but maybe I'll have a cup of tea." The housekeeper took a seat and placed her black handbag at her feet. Then she glanced at her wristwatch. "From what I understand, the meeting is in an hour. Will you have time to eat, change clothes and drive to the office?"

"I'm only going to have a salad," Chloe said. "And I'm already dressed."

The woman's brow twitched and her lips tensed. She fingered the silver cross on her necklace. "I see."

Apparently she didn't agree with Chloe's choice of apparel—a form-fitting black dress. The stuffy/snobby type rarely did. But then again, Desiree had given the woman her stamp of approval, so Chloe would reserve judgment.

"I suppose it might be more appropriate to wear something a bit more conservative," Chloe admitted. "But I gave up dressing to impress others years ago."

And she had the emotional scars to prove it, although she kept them hidden. Still, every now and again, they crept to the forefront, reminding her of who she was and where she'd come from.

In spite of the money her father had managed to parlay in his dealings and the prestigious private school he'd sent her to, life had been tough for her as a child. Her classmates at Preston Prep had not only been cliquish, but mean. And no matter how hard Chloe had tried to conform, dressing to their standards, it hadn't mattered one bit. So she'd given up and had decided to wear whatever she darned well pleased.

Either way, the boys seemed to flock around her. And she'd soon learned how to use that to her advantage—advice she'd learned from Desiree, actually.

Lessons from Desiree #2: "Be proud of your assets and make the best of them."

Chloe had not only taken that bit of wisdom to heart, she'd also put her own spin on it: if you've got it, flaunt it.

"You look pretty," Brianna said. "Just like Mommy."

Chloe cupped the child's cheek. "Thanks, honey. I can't think of a nicer compliment than that."

Over lunch, Brianna chattered away about the friends she'd met in Bayside, as well as her visits to the San Diego Zoo and Sea World.

"I'm glad you had a good time," Barbara said. "I plan to take my niece and nephew on a trip someday. Maybe I ought to consider the San Diego area."

Twenty minutes later, after finishing the last of her salad, Chloe blotted her lips with the napkin, then reached for her purse and gave Mrs. Davies the key to their room. "We're in 1410."

"Are you going now?" Brianna asked.

"I need to visit the ladies' room first and freshen my makeup. Then I'm off so I can get this meeting out of the way." Chloe didn't need to look at Mrs. Davies to sense the woman's disapproval, yet old habits were tough to break, and she stole a peek anyway.

Yep. Brow furrowed, expression severe.

Over the years, and after innumerable disappointments, Chloe no longer gave a rip about what people thought of her, but sometimes, the lonely child within couldn't refrain from seeking approval and respect.

But there was no way on earth she'd try to be someone or something she wasn't. Not today. So she'd made up her mind to pull out all the stops when it came to dressing for this meeting. She'd done it for Desiree.

And for herself.

"Brian Willoughby and Jake Braddock are both rather conventional," Mrs. Davies said.

"Good." Chloe couldn't help but smile as she scooted her chair back and stood. "Then this meeting ought to be interesting."

"To say the least," the older woman responded.

"Have fun with Mrs. Davies," Chloe told Brianna. Then she placed a kiss on the little girl's cheek, leaving a faint pink mark. "I'll be back as soon as I can."

As she strode toward the restroom, she tugged at the hem of the knit dress that had hiked up when she'd been sitting. It was something she'd wear clubbing, if she were inclined to do that sort of thing. As it was, even though she owned the proper nighttime wardrobe, her evenings were pretty quiet. Or as Desiree would say, pleasantly boring.

Chloe ought to be nervous about facing Jake Braddock again, she supposed. But sometimes it was fun to be a bit naughty and rebellious.

Especially around conservative men who valued being in control of those around them.

Jake sat in Willoughby's office, waiting for Desiree's "dear" friend to arrive. He glanced at his watch. 1:32 p.m.

Some women didn't consider themselves late until fifteen minutes had passed, but punctuality was important to him.

And Chloe Haskell was late.

When a buzz sounded on the intercom, the attorney responded. "Yes."

"Ms. Haskell is here," a woman's voice said.

"Please show her in."

Willoughby stood, and Jake followed suit. But when the attractive redhead swept into the room, wearing a curve-hugging, black knit dress and spike heels, Jake nearly dropped back in his seat.

Mercy. At any moment he expected to hear music in the background and Roy Orbison break out in song at the sight of her.

Hands down, Chloe was a hell of a pretty woman.

And too damn sexy for words.

"Please have a seat," Willoughby said.

"Thank you." She moved toward the chair next to

Jake with the grace of a dancer, her eyes glimmering with sexual confidence.

Jake might have braced himself for a fight, but he hadn't realized he'd have to buck his libido, too.

Interestingly, Willoughby didn't seem to be the least bit fazed by her. And why was that?

Jake supposed it was because Desiree had always carried herself in a similar manner, and her attorney had grown used to it.

Well, Jake wouldn't get used to it. Looking at Chloe all dolled up like that left him a bit unbalanced. And he didn't like having the urge to stare.

Fortunately, Willoughby got them all back on track by reading the will. And per Desiree's wishes, the estate was split between Jake and Brianna, which Jake didn't have a problem with. But Desiree had appointed Chloe to look after Brianna's holdings and her best interests until she was of age.

What kind of ogre had Desiree thought he was?

Jake would never put his own interests ahead of his sister's, so his stepmother's distrust cut him to the quick.

Chloe shifted in her seat, drawing his attention, then crossed a leg over her knee, flashing a lovely stretch of thigh. "What about custody of Brianna?"

Jake tore his gaze away from the sexy redhead and focused on the attorney. Chloe had only been granted *temporary* custody. Surely, Desiree knew the best person to have permanent custody was Jake.

"Desiree appointed you two as joint guardians," Willoughby said.

"Excuse me?" Jake gripped the armrests of his leather seat. "That's crazy. Desiree couldn't have been in her right mind when she drew up that document. How in blazes can two people living in different states share custody of a child who will start kindergarten in the fall?"

"Let me read the letter she wrote, giving the details of her wishes." Willoughby sorted through the pages before him, found what he was looking for and cleared his throat:

"Dear Jake and Chloe,

I've been dealt a crappy hand, but I'll play it out to the end. I know this may be a bit out of the ordinary, but I hope you'll understand where I'm coming from.

Brianna has lost her father and now me. No child should have to go through that, but I've tried to prepare her the best I can. Now it's up to you. I know that you both love her. And interestingly enough, I believe that having the two of you share custody will be best for her. Jake, you favor your father in more ways than looks. And Chloe, you're a lot like me. I'm hopeful that Brianna will be comforted by that.

I'm asking you to live together as a family at the ranch for six weeks. At the end of that time, I'd like you both to come to an agreement on how to make shared custody work."

What? No way.

Jake wasn't about to stay in the same house with a sexy redheaded bombshell who seemed to get off on taunting a man.

Willoughby continued to read:

> *"I realize you both are established in separate states, but maybe Brianna can spend the school year in Bayside and summer vacations, holidays and some weekends on the ranch. Either way, I know you both love her. And I expect you to learn to accept each other and become friends for Brianna's sake."*

"A request like that can't be legally binding," Jake said.

"You're right." Willoughby placed the letter on his desk, then folded his hands over the handwritten note. "You don't have to abide by her wishes, but she hoped you would agree for Brianna's sake. It was Desiree's sole desire to ease her daughter's loss and help her to adjust to life without her parents. In fact, that's why Brianna has been seeing a child psychologist in town for weekly visits, something Desiree also hoped you two will continue for a while."

"Desiree explained her wishes to me weeks ago," Chloe said. "And as difficult as it will be for me to remain in Texas, I promised her I would do so."

"Well, she didn't say squat to me," Jake snapped.

"I didn't even know she had cancer. Or that she was dying."

"Jake," Willoughby said, "what's done is done. But if Desiree told me once, she told me a dozen times. She wished the two of you had been closer."

Jake raked a hand through his hair. Okay, so he'd been a bit…hardheaded. What would it have hurt to be…well, not friends, but…

He blew out a sigh. He should have taken the olive branch she'd tried to give him, but it was too damn late to do anything about it now. Either way, he wasn't going to reveal his regret here. Or anywhere, for that matter.

"Desiree also asked that you return here in six weeks with your decision," Willoughby added. "And, at that time, if you can't agree, a preappointed third party is to evaluate the relationship between the child and each adult and determine who should be granted full custody, with fair visitation given to the other."

"Who is the third party?" Jake asked.

"Desiree asked that the identity be kept secret so that there was no chance of influencing the decision. Of course, Mrs. Braddock was hopeful that it wouldn't come to that."

Jake suspected the psychologist was the person who would make the ultimate decision on custody. It only made sense. And, that being the case, maybe Jake ought to volunteer to take Brianna to her appointments so he could share his concerns with the doctor about Chloe's ability to parent.

Willoughby reached into a manila envelope, withdrew something small and handed it to Chloe. "Here's the key to the ranch."

A chill hunkered over Jake, as he watched his father's memories and essence be given to a stranger—at least, symbolically.

And what about Brianna?

Who would make sure she was okay during all of this?

Damn.

As it was, he had no choice but to agree with his stepmother's foolish request to move back to the ranch temporarily. If they were all together, it would be easier for Jake to look out for Brianna's best interests and make sure she was treated well.

And if she wasn't?

Then he'd have firsthand evidence for the custody battle he would wage when Desiree's fantasy family failed.

Chapter Three

The next morning Jake packed his bags, then threw them in the back of his Lincoln Navigator and headed for the ranch.

During the entire one-hour-and-fifteen-minute drive out of the city, he utilized his cell phone, informing his office staff and rescheduling as many meetings as possible. He'd do what he could from a distance, but there would be days when he'd have no choice but to make the trek back to Dallas.

Damn. His life would be out of whack for six long weeks.

Desiree had surely been out of her ever-loving mind when she'd cooked up this scheme. Not that he wouldn't have put his life on hold indefinitely for

Brianna or done whatever it took to make sure she adjusted to her loss. But he couldn't figure out why Desiree had thrown Chloe into the mix. It hadn't been necessary—unless this was some lame attempt to punish Jake. Of course, if she'd known how much he now regretted not coming around more often, she wouldn't have bothered. His conscience would be punishing him for a long time to come.

Up ahead he spotted the entrance to the ranch and turned on his left blinker. Then he swung into the tree-lined, graveled drive and continued to the house.

The wooden fence, which surrounded the front portion of the property from the county road, had been bright white when his father had been alive, but it needed a fresh coat of paint. He'd have to see that it got done, because when the designated time passed and the custody issue had been settled, he was going to put this place on the market, something his father should have done years ago.

The Braddock Enterprises office was in the city, as was Jake's townhouse, so there was no reason to keep the ranch.

He parked his SUV near the barn, removed his things—a leather briefcase and an overnight bag—then headed toward the front porch of the sprawling custom-built adobe house. His first inclination had been to open the front door without knocking, something he'd done when only his father had lived here. But times had changed.

As he climbed the front porch steps, the morning

sun moved from behind a cloud, casting its light over him. A westerly breeze kicked up, and he caught a whiff of alfalfa. In the distance, a horse whinnied.

He almost felt like a kid again. Coming home.

But that couldn't be further from the truth. The ranch had ceased being a home to him the day Desiree had moved in. The day his father had become another person.

Jake knocked lightly, and when no one responded, he rang the bell. It was discomfiting to know there was a stranger living here—even temporarily.

Footsteps from within sounded, and Barbara Davies, the housekeeper, answered the door.

He lifted the briefcase he held in one hand and the suitcase he held in the other. "Desiree's orders."

"Yes, I know." She stepped aside, allowing him entrance. "She mentioned it to me a month or two ago."

Again Jake was reminded that he hadn't been privy to squat. And since he was probably to blame for refusing his stepmother's offers of friendship, another rush of regret twisted a knot in his gut. There wasn't much he could do about it now, though.

"Would you like to stay in the master bedroom?" Barbara asked. "I've got it ready for you."

Since that room had been the one his father had shared with Desiree, and then hers alone, he wouldn't feel comfortable in there. "No, I think I'll stay in my own bedroom, the one I used as a kid."

After his folks had split up, Jake lived with his dad, who insisted upon spending every weekend at the ranch to give his city-boy son a wholesome dose of reality.

There'd been some good times, Jake supposed, remembering the old fishing hole, horseback riding. But there'd been chores, too. Mucking out stalls, shoveling horse manure.

"Consider them character-building tasks," his father had often said.

At the time Jake had been skeptical. He still was, he supposed.

As Mrs. Davies closed the door behind him, he was pulled from the nostalgic past and forced back to the awkward present.

He scanned the living room, the leather furniture, the oak and glass-topped tables and shelves, the stone fireplace with its rough-hewn mantel, the colorful Southwestern art on white plastered walls. Desiree had redecorated when she'd moved in, but she hadn't changed much since then.

"From what I understand," the housekeeper said, "your old room is just the way you left it. I dust it twice a week, and although the sheets are clean, the bedding needs to be freshened. I'll do that later this morning."

"Don't worry about it."

"I take pride in my work," she said. "And it's no trouble at all."

The warm aroma of cinnamon and spice drifted in from the kitchen, and his stomach rumbled, reminding him he'd only had an espresso earlier. "Something sure smells good."

Mrs. Davies beamed. "It's the zucchini muffins in the oven. Desiree told me you liked them. And they're almost ready."

How would Desiree have known that? he wondered. Had he mentioned it to her once? If so, it was odd that she'd remember. And that she'd pass that tidbit of information along.

On the other hand, he didn't have a clue as to what kind of things Desiree had liked. He'd never noticed, never cared. And although it hadn't bothered him before, he felt a bit remiss right now.

"I've made a lemon meringue pie, too," the housekeeper added.

Another favorite of Jake's.

It was as though Desiree was trying hard to make him feel welcomed, yet instead her efforts—or rather her predeath orders—only made him…uneasy. And undeserving.

"It's pretty quiet in here," he said, trying his best to shrug off his discomfort.

"Everyone else is still asleep."

He glanced at his watch—10:07 a.m. Apparently, Chloe was a night owl. A lot of prima donnas were. He hoped that kind of attitude didn't rub off on his little sister.

"How's Brianna doing?" he asked.

"Last night was a bit rough. She had a crying spell, then had a difficult time falling asleep. Chloe read to her until at least eleven, which is when I finally turned in."

Okay, so maybe he'd been wrong about the prima donna thing—at least, last night.

At the sound of footsteps padding along the hallway, Jake spotted Chloe entering the living room wearing a white sleeveless undershirt and low-riding sweatpants.

She yawned, then ran a hand through her tousled hair, an acrylic nail snagging on a rumpled red curl.

Seeing her like that, fresh out of bed, was more arousing that he cared to admit. And even though she was fairly well covered, she looked as sexy as hell, and he couldn't keep his eyes off her.

He wanted to suggest she go back and put on a robe, but wouldn't. No need for her to suspect the kind of effect she had on him.

"Good morning," the housekeeper said, her voice as tight as the rubber band in a cocked and primed slingshot. "Now that you're up, I'll put on a pot of coffee and whip up some breakfast."

"Thank you," Chloe said. "I'm not much of an eater in the morning, but I'd love a cup of coffee."

When they were alone, Jake set his bags on the floor and crossed his arms. It was time to lay it on the line, to find out what Chloe's thoughts were about all of this and what he was up against. "I imagine that you aren't any happier about things than I am."

Chloe met his stare, lifting her chin a little. "You're right." She wasn't at all pleased about leaving her dance studio and relying on someone else to look after her rental properties. And she wasn't especially comfortable living in someone else's house and having a live-in housekeeper/cook, either.

Mrs. Davies was nice enough, but she had an innate way of lifting her nose and arching a brow whenever Chloe did or said anything she considered unconventional. And since Chloe never paid much attention to social mores, the older woman's nose and brow seemed to be in constant motion.

Then, to make matters worse, she had to deal with a man who was too conservative for his own good, a man she suspected would try to control her every chance he got.

She strode toward the cream-colored leather sofa and sat on the armrest. "But do you know what? If I had asked Desiree to make a sacrifice for me, she wouldn't have thought twice about doing so."

Jake didn't respond.

"And whether you believe it or not," Chloe added, "Desiree would have done the same for you."

"We weren't that close," he said.

"I know. And I'm sorry for your loss. It was huge."

He studied her for a moment with those baby-blue eyes that suggested a softness she doubted he had. "You're probably right about that."

His agreement took her aback, and she tucked an unruly strand of hair behind her ear.

"What did she tell you about me?" he asked, watching her intently. Too intently.

"Not much. Just that you reminded her of your father, a man she adored. And that she'd give anything to make you feel comfortable enough to visit the ranch more often."

"I was busy."

"She'd said that, too."

He shifted his weight to one foot. "I made it for Christmas and holidays. It's not like I was a complete stranger."

Token visits, Desiree had told Chloe. And if she'd ever had any regrets about her marriage to Gerald Braddock, it was the fact that she'd unintentionally caused a rift of sorts between father and son.

"What else?" Jake asked.

"Actually, we didn't discuss you all that much. I'd heard you were driven. And stubborn. But that you were handsome, too. Is that what you meant?"

He squirmed a bit at the physical description, which she couldn't help spouting, even though it hadn't really come up. But since Desiree had said he looked like his father, and Gerald Braddock was a gorgeous older man, Chloe had put two and two together.

However, her addition had come up short. She hadn't realized just how attractive Jake was. How appealing she might find him. Or how she might, under different circumstances, be tempted to…well, maybe not pursue him romantically. But flirting was always fun.

She'd learned early on that men like him weren't the kind to pin her heart on. Of course, she wasn't sure just what type of man was the kind she could trust for the long haul.

"For what it's worth," Jake said, "I don't know what negative things Desiree may have said about me, but I'm not a bad guy."

Not entirely, Chloe supposed, but Desiree must have had a good reason not to give him full custody of Brianna.

"You don't believe me?" he asked.

"Sure I do." She tried to force sincerity into her smile, yet a veil of skepticism slid over his angular face.

He didn't object, which she appreciated. She wasn't up for a confrontation until after she'd had her morning coffee.

Still, her temporary housemate could be considered eye candy, with dark curly hair that brushed his collar, a complexion that suggested some Latin blood and eyes the color of Mission Bay.

Too bad he was so stuffy.

A rebellious spirit she sometimes used as a defensive ploy swept over her, and she decided to flirt and make him squirm—a game she'd played for years. Of course, she'd only mess with him like that when Brianna wasn't around.

Before she could conjure a teasing remark, Barbara entered the room. "Coffee's ready."

"Good." Chloe slid from her seat on the armrest and followed the housekeeper back to the kitchen.

She'd have to put the flirting on hold for the time being and take care of her morning caffeine addiction.

Yet, in spite of her craving for a hot cup of java,

she glanced over her shoulder, only to find Jake rooted to the spot in which she'd left him, eyes locked on her. Or rather on her fanny, since his gaze had to travel upward to meet hers.

Apparently, she would be able to tease him without even trying, and a grin tugged at her lips. "Are you coming?"

"Not yet. I'm going to put away my things first."

"Suit yourself."

"I always do."

She nodded, a full-on smile busting free, as she returned to her quest for coffee.

Jake Braddock would be fun and easy to taunt, but he probably wouldn't be a good sport about it, which meant he was her favorite type of male challenge.

And he'd just thrown down the gauntlet.

Later that morning, after taking a walk out to the barn and talking to the ranch foreman, Jake returned to the house and headed into his father's office, only to find Chloe seated at the desk, an open phonebook in front of her.

She'd showered and changed. Her hair, once wild and free, had been swept into a twist. And she'd applied makeup, which some women needed but she didn't. That's the conclusion he'd easily come to this morning, when he'd seen her fresh out of bed.

She had a wholesome beauty about her. Too bad she didn't realize a cosmetic company couldn't bottle and sell what she'd been blessed with.

Her dark pink lipstick had been applied carefully—and thick. She wore it in a way that would definitely smear when a man kissed her. And for a moment he wondered if she did that on purpose. To keep men at bay.

Come here, big boy. But keep your distance.

He leaned against the doorjamb, studying her until curiosity got the better of him. "What are you doing?"

She glanced up. "Checking on something and getting an address. As soon as Brianna finishes her breakfast, I'm going to take her into town."

"You mean the city?" he asked. Dallas was more than an hour away.

"No. Into Granger. How far is it from here?"

"About ten miles."

She didn't seem to be the small-town type. And even though he didn't like people prying into his life, his plans, he couldn't help himself from wondering what she was up to. But, hey, that's only because she wanted to take Brianna with her. "What are you going to do in Granger?"

Her green eyes glimmered like those of a child who'd just been told the bus was heading to Seven Flags Over Texas for the day, rather than school. "I'm going to do some window shopping."

Okay, so she wasn't the open and talkative sort. "For what?"

"I'm not sure yet. Let's just say it's a surprise."

Oh, yeah? Jake didn't like surprises. And it made him suspicious, something else he didn't like.

Maybe she planned a shopping spree for herself, rather than Brianna.

Well, if that was the case, he'd put a stop to that pretty damn quick, especially if she planned to use money from the trust. Braddock Enterprises wasn't going to support Chloe and her spending whims.

She closed the phonebook and put it back in the drawer. Then she stood, a pair of black jeans fitting like a sleek leather glove. "Don't worry. We'll be back in an hour."

Well, he *was* worried.

But then again, he didn't need to be. Not if he followed her into town.

"Suit yourself," he said.

"I always do." She tossed his own line back at him along with a playful grin, then swept out of the office, her denim-clad hips swaying as she headed for the kitchen.

Six friggin' weeks. She'd drive him nuts by then— if he let her.

Twenty minutes later Jake had followed Chloe and Brianna into town and now waited in front of the Granger Animal Shelter.

He had no idea what in the world they were doing inside, but he had a suspicion. She'd said she was merely window shopping, and he hoped that was her game plan. She'd better not be getting a pet, not if Jake was the one who'd be taking full custody of Brianna.

Curiosity got the better of him, and just as he

reached for the door handle to let himself out of his vehicle, Chloe and Brianna walked out the front door.

Chloe carried a cardboard box with holes.

Oh, for Pete's sake. He climbed out of the Navigator and made his way toward them.

"Jake!" Brianna said. "Guess what we have!"

Instead of guessing, he focused on Chloe, on the sunglasses that hid her eyes, on the dimples her grin created.

"What a surprise," she said. "We didn't expect you to follow us."

"No, I'm sure you didn't." He nodded toward the box. "I suppose *that's* the surprise."

Brianna grinned from ear to ear. "Want to see him?"

The fact that the critter, whatever it was, had placed the bright-eyed smile on his sister's face was reason enough to make him back down. And even though something like a pet adoption should have been discussed with him first, it was a relief to know their purchase was small enough to fit in that box.

"His name is Sweetie Pie," Brianna said. "And he's the bestest dog in the whole, wide world."

Jake didn't have the heart to tell her no.

Chloe unhooked the edge of the box, allowing it to open, and a mangy, wire-haired, tri-color dog poked its head out, whimpering and squirming, its tail beating against the cardboard container.

"Oops," Chloe said, juggling the box. "Settle down, Sweetie Pie. You'll make me drop you."

"We have to keep him in the box until we get back

to the ranch," Brianna said. "That's the rules. But once he's at home, he gets to run around all he wants."

As Chloe struggled to tuck the scraggly dog back into the cardboard carrier, Jake opened the back door of the car for his sister. She climbed into her seat, and he secured her. Then Chloe put the box on the rear floorboard.

Once the door was shut, his redheaded nemesis crossed her arms and arched an auburn brow. "So, you couldn't help but follow us, huh?"

"I don't like secrets."

"Too bad. You've probably had some boring birthdays, then."

"They were just fine." Truth be told, he'd never had a surprise party, if that's what she was getting at. And she made it sound as though he'd missed something. "So what's the deal with the dog?"

"All kids need a pet."

"Oh, yeah? Don't you think they should be old enough and responsible enough to take care of them? Of course, if you're planning to transport that dog back to California with you in six weeks, I'll keep quiet."

"Sweetie Pie will go wherever Brianna goes."

"Then I'll have to kiss up to Mrs. Davies, since she'll be the one looking after the dog for me."

"That's left to be seen."

They were heading for a face-off, which wasn't appropriate here and now. A glance into the backseat told him Brianna was happy with her pet, so he decided not to make an issue out of it…yet.

"By the way," Jake said, as Chloe turned to open the driver's door of her car. "That's the ugliest mutt I've ever seen. If you're going to turn the ranch into a zoo, why not choose a better-looking critter?"

Her motions slowed, and she turned to face him again, her stance softening this time. Their gazes locked, and her eyes glistened. If he didn't know better, he'd suspect she was tearing up. Hell, maybe she was.

The breeze sent a strand of her hair across her cheek and she brushed it aside. She cleared her throat, and her voice came out softer than he expected. "Because that little dog needed a home more than the rest of them. His number was up today."

Jake had never been an animal person. Well, not as a grown-up, anyway. He'd found a stray shepherd-mix once, but his mom had refused to let him keep it. And he couldn't blame her. She lived in a town house in the city.

And so did he.

"That dog—" he began.

"Sweetie Pie," Chloe corrected. "He has a name."

Jake crossed his arms. "Either way, my place isn't geared for pets."

She leaned her hip against the car door and crossed her own arms. "Whatever."

Damn that woman. She was going to be the death of him.

"Listen," she said, softening again, it seemed. "A pet will be good for Brianna. Especially now."

"She already has fish."

"She can't cuddle with them."

"Yeah, well, she won't get flea bites from them, either."

Chloe stood there for a moment, eyes glaring and rigidity returning to her stance. Then she chuckled softly. "Six weeks won't be long enough, will it?"

It seemed too long to him. But he wasn't entirely sure what she meant. "What are you talking about?"

"You and I are going to have a heck of a time learning how to compromise and put Brianna's best interests ahead of our own." Then she tossed him another smile and climbed into the car.

Jake stood silently by, as he watched her drive away.

Something told him she was right.

Even so, he realized, in spite of his objections and reservations, Brianna was sitting in Chloe's backseat. And that ugly dog was heading back to the ranch.

So how come it felt more like a loss than a compromise?

And what was he going to do about it?

Chapter Four

Once back at the ranch, Chloe took Brianna and the dog to the guest bathroom, where they filled the tub.

The man at the shelter insisted all the animals had been treated with flea dip, but Chloe wanted to wash the doggie smell from Sweetie Pie—especially since he would be living indoors.

"Wait until we get him all cleaned up," Chloe told Brianna. "You won't be able to recognize him."

Brianna wrapped her arms around the scruffy dog and hugged it close. "You're going to love this, Sweetie Pie."

The fidgety dog, its head cocked to one side and its tail pounding the floor to beat the band, didn't appear the least bit convinced.

Chloe reached into the flow of water and decided the temperature was just right. "Brianna, can you please open the cupboard under the sink and pull out my shampoo and conditioner? They're in two shiny black bottles."

The child did as she was told, then asked, "Can I open them?"

"Sure. Go ahead and take a whiff while you're at it. I love the scent."

"Mmm." Brianna smiled. "It smells pretty, just like you."

"Thanks, Breezy."

A knock sounded at the bathroom door, then Jake's voice rang out with a grumpy tone. "What's going on in there?"

Chloe suspected he was more perturbed at being out of the loop than actually curious about what they were doing with the dog. "Please don't open the door. We're giving Sweetie Pie a bath, and he's not sure he wants to go through with it."

A masculine grumble erupted, followed by fading footsteps, and Chloe couldn't help but grin. It was going to be easy to ruffle the stuffy Texan's feathers—if she wanted to.

And if truth be told?

Stirring the pot was a game she liked to play.

As a child, she'd learned that she was different from the other kids. Not because she had Little Orphan Annie hair, a sprinkle of freckles across her nose or big green eyes, but because the people she'd come to love and think of as family weren't respected in society. And even though her father, who'd parlayed his winnings into lucrative real estate ventures, had been able to give Chloe everything money could buy, he hadn't been able to provide her with the social acceptance she'd once craved.

Her father had insisted that it was just a matter of time. Believing that money was an amazing equalizer, he'd insisted she attend a prestigious private school in the San Diego area, hoping she'd find her rightful place in society. And no matter how hard she'd tried to tell him, he'd had no idea how exclusive the kids at Preston Prep had been, how malicious. And no matter how hard Chloe had tried to conform, dressing up to their standards, it hadn't mattered one bit. They'd pointed at her and whispered anyway.

So, in the end, she'd decided to take the power position, to be proud of her seedy background, to lift her head high and give them something to gossip about. With Desiree as her coach, she'd dressed to attract attention and it had certainly worked.

She hadn't had any real girlfriends, but the boys had certainly flocked around her. It hadn't taken long to learn they had only one thing in mind, which she wasn't about to give up to just anyone—another lesson she'd learned from Desiree.

"Don't make the same mistakes I did," Desiree had told her. "Don't sleep with any guy you wouldn't want to be the daddy to your children."

Chloe glanced at Brianna, at a child born of love. "What do you think, Breezy? Is the water in the tub deep enough?"

The girl nodded. "Should I get in with him?"

"Not this time." Chloe scooped the little mutt into her arms and slowly lowered him into the water. "Okay, Sweetie Pie. It's time for your bath. We'll have you looking and smelling like you just stepped out of the finest hair salon in town."

Not many people would bathe a dog with such an expensive product, but this particular brand worked wonders on Chloe's curls, so it should take out the snarls and tangles from the dog's fur. Besides, poor little Sweetie Pie had been neglected for too long and deserved the best.

Chloe applied a dollop of luxurious shampoo and began to lather it into the dog's coat. All the while she cooed and tried to calm the squirmy animal.

As Chloe worked carefully to wash the fur around the dog's head without getting it into his face, Brianna said, "Oh, look. Sweetie Pie has really big eyes. I couldn't even see them before. His bangs are *way* too long. Maybe we need to give him a haircut, too."

"The scruffy look on doggies is in this season." Chloe thought about Antoine, her stylist, and wondered what he'd say if he knew she was using her fifty-dollar-a-bottle shampoo on a stray she'd just picked up from the pound. "But I have an idea, Breezy. Maybe, after we blow him dry, we can use one of your barrettes to pull a little bit of his hair out of his face."

"I know which one we can use!" Brianna jumped up and dashed out of the bathroom.

As Chloe turned to watch the child go, her grip on the dog loosened. As though waiting for an opportunity to escape, Sweetie Pie jumped away and scrambled from the tub. Chloe tried to grab him, going so far as to pull him against her chest, but the slick little dog wriggled away and tore out of the bathroom, stopping briefly to shake the soap and water from his head to his tail. Then he scampered through the house.

Chloe, her blouse wet, cold and sticking to her skin, jumped up and hurried after the dog. "Brianna! Come quick. We've got a problem."

But it wasn't Brianna who responded to her plea.

Jake poked his head out of the office door, where he'd holed up after they'd gotten back from the animal shelter.

"What the hell…" His bewildered expression was priceless.

"The dog. It got away." Hoping to diffuse Jake's exasperation, Chloe stopped, tossed up her hands and shrugged. "He's a spunky little thing and ought to make a great pet."

Jake's focus traveled from Chloe's face to her chest, and as she followed his gaze she realized why. The material of her blouse, now wet and see-through, revealed the dainty white pushup bra underneath. She'd developed a respectable pair of breasts early, and so she'd always chosen bras to enhance what she'd been blessed with.

Still, the flash of lace and the hint of skin hadn't been intentional, but as Jake arched a brow, she fig–ured he thought it had been. As their eyes met again, sexual awareness buzzed between them—something Chloe wasn't particularly happy about.

She didn't mind flirting with cocky guys who thought they were better than her, but she never messed around with the ones she found attractive. She'd done that once and had been burned. And with her track record, she wasn't going to risk a bruised ego or allow her feelings to be hurt by a man who wanted something different from a relationship than she did.

So, she tore her gaze away from Jake—her way-ward musings, too. "If you'll excuse me, I've got to get the dog."

He leaned against the doorjamb. "You know, this serves you right for bringing that mutt home in the first place. It was a big mistake."

"That's left to be seen."

"Is it?" He glanced down at the watery, soap-laced paw-print splatters left on the hardwood floor.

Chloe was going to argue and insist that Brianna needed a pet, that all children did, but now wasn't the time. "You can either help us catch the dog or turn around and go back in the office and stay out of the way."

"I'm *not* giving that animal a bath." Jake slapped his hands on his hips. "And even if I'd been part of the fool purchase and adoption of the little mutt, I don't take orders from anyone."

If she'd had something within arm's distance, she might have thrown it at him, regardless of its size, shape or value.

"Will someone *please* help me?" Brianna asked from the arched doorway that led to the living room. Chloe and Jake both turned to see the girl seated on the floor, holding the wet, lathered dog in her arms. "Sweetie Pie is going to get away again."

As Jake strode toward his little sister, he grumbled under his breath. He'd meant everything he'd said about not helping with the dog, but he couldn't let Brianna wrestle the little beast alone. He blew out a ragged sigh, then stooped to pick up the mongrel. With his arms extended, he carried it back to the bathroom.

Dang. The little critter smelled just like Chloe. "What kind of soap did you put on him?"

"It's not soap," Brianna said. "It's special shampoo for pretty ladies. Doesn't it smell good?"

"It smells expensive." And a whole lot better on Chloe than it did on the dog.

Once he'd deposited Sweetie Pie in the tub, he returned to the hallway and snatched a couple of towels from the linen closet. Then he proceeded to mop up the water. All the while he grumbled about crazy mutts, wild-ass schemes and women set on destroying a man's peaceful existence.

By the time he'd gotten the mess cleaned up and

deposited the damp towels in the laundry room, he heard the slow, steady hum of a blow dryer. Wouldn't you know it? Chloe and Brianna were playing beauty shop with the dog and treating it like a king.

If Brianna hadn't been so blasted happy about having a new pet, he would have put his foot down. As it was, he hadn't had the heart.

Twenty minutes later Chloe and Brianna brought Sweetie Pie into the office, where Jake had been working online. A long, red ribbon had been tied to the generic brown collar the critter had worn at the pound.

"See?" Brianna said, pointing to what looked like a completely different animal than the one they'd brought home. "Isn't he cute?"

Jake wouldn't go that far, but with a blue barrette pulling a strand of the shaggy hair from its eyes, it now resembled a well-loved pet. "Granted, the dog looks better, but you two are a mess."

Brianna laughed. "You can play with Sweetie Pie while we clean up."

"I'm not a dogsitter."

Chloe crossed her arms. Her wet blouse wasn't nearly as revealing as it had been earlier, but he could still see the swell of her breasts as they strained against that skimpy bra she wore.

He jerked his attention back to the dog. "All that mutt needs now is a manicure and pedicure."

His comment and tone couldn't have been any more sarcastic, but Chloe brightened.

"That's a great idea." She turned to Brianna. "I have some red fingernail polish in my makeup bag."

"Oh, for Pete's sake," Jake muttered as they dashed out with Sweetie Pie on their heels, leaving him alone in the office.

But not as alone as he'd prefer to be.

Desiree had surely been out of her ever-lovin' mind when she came up with the fantasy family idea. And six weeks of her cock-and-bull game plan was going to drive him to drink before it was all said and done—unless he did something about it.

Tonight, after Brianna went to bed, Jake would confront Chloe and lay down some ground rules.

Working away from the office was a pain, even with a laptop computer that was networked with the other systems at Braddock Enterprises. Still Jake gave it his best shot all afternoon—until the warm aroma of baked chicken filled the house. His stomach growled, reminding him he'd worked through lunch.

He glanced at the clock resting on a built-in walnut bookcase—6:03 p.m. Dinner would be ready soon. He signed off and shut down the computer for the night.

As he walked out of the office, the guest-room door swung open and Chloe stepped into the hallway. Her lips parted when she saw him, so he figured she hadn't expected to run into him, either.

Her hair had been pulled into a ponytail, but

some of the curls that framed her face refused to be tamed. The easy, casual style suited her, he supposed. Sexy and wild.

She wore a pink T-shirt that was stretched to the limit. Not that it was too small. It was just…made with her body in mind. The cotton-candy color made her the epitome of eye candy and a real temptation for a man's…blood sugar level. And so were those tight-fitting jeans.

"Don't you have a pair of baggy cargo pants and an oversized blouse you can wear?" he asked.

She glanced down at her shirt. "What's wrong with this?"

Nothing, he supposed, but the way she was packaged in her clothes had his hormones warring with his common sense. "It's not the kind of thing you ought to be wearing on a ranch."

"Is that right?" She placed a hand on a shapely hip, shifted her weight to one leg and tapped a pretty, bare foot adorned with hot-pink nail polish.

He managed a nod.

"I beg to differ." A wry grin tugged at her lips. "Just to get acclimated to Texas ranch life, I watched CMT nonstop for a week. And I think I fit right in. All I need is a cowboy hat and a pair of boots."

"Hot pink, no doubt."

He expected a snappy retort, a snide response. Instead she lowered her voice to a suggestive whisper. "If you can't stand the heat of my wardrobe, take a cold shower."

Yeah, well, if she didn't start dressing more modestly, he'd have to stay under a spray of ice water until his skin turned blue and wrinkled. But he'd be damned if he'd let her know that.

"I don't care what you wear," he lied. "But my sister is young and easily influenced."

"Actually, she's not the least bit interested in what I wear. Right now she's big on castles and princesses. If you'd spent more time with her or taken her shopping, you'd know that."

"I've been swamped at the office, although I'm hopeful that will change. And speaking of shopping, on your last spree you apparently decided she needed a dog more than anything else."

"No," Chloe said, "that's not true. She needs her mommy and daddy more than anything else. You and I and the dog are merely substitutes."

How did she do that? Change the focus of the conversation from sex and modesty to family and grief?

"Dinner's ready," Mrs. Davies called from the kitchen."

"Good. I'm starving." Chloe headed to the dining room, leaving Jake to follow up the rear. Or rather *her* rear.

She walked with a sexy sway of her hips. It wasn't so pronounced that he could swear it was deliberate, but it damn near seemed that way.

Could a woman learn to walk like that without a whole lot of practice?

"Yum," Chloe said, as she approached.

Mrs. Davies was placing a pitcher of iced tea on the table. She smiled and smoothed the front of her apron. "It's just a little something I threw together."

Jake scanned the platter of golden-baked chicken, scalloped potatoes, creamed corn and a tossed salad with what appeared to be homemade buttermilk ranch dressing. That "little something," Jake decided, was quite a spread. "What's in the covered basket?

"Warm cornbread," the woman said proudly.

"Where's Brianna?" Chloe asked.

"Here I am." The child entered the room with Sweetie Pie still tethered to a length of red ribbon.

Jake nodded at the mutt. "That dog needs to go outside while we eat."

"But, Jake," Brianna said, "we can't turn him loose. He'll get lost or be scared all by himself."

"That's right." Chloe crossed her arms in what seemed to be her habit when challenging Jake and shifted her weight to that same pretty foot. "Even if Sweetie Pie wasn't going to be a house dog—and he *is*—we can't let him outside. He doesn't have street smarts."

Jake was sure he didn't. Otherwise, he wouldn't have gotten nabbed by the dogcatcher in the first place.

"He was a stray," Chloe added. "An elderly man found him hiding beneath a tree during a thunderstorm, shaking from cold and fear. So the man rescued him and took him to the shelter."

"So we *can't* let him go outside," Brianna said.

Mrs. Davies took the ribbon from Brianna's hand. "Why don't I put the dog on the service porch? You can come and get him as soon as you're finished eating."

It seemed as though they'd reached a compromise. So they sat at the table, which had been set family style, although they couldn't have been any less of one. And other than an occasional whine from the dog out on the porch, they ate in silence.

When they began to dig into slices of homemade German-chocolate cake for dessert, Mrs. Davies picked up the serving dishes and took them back to the kitchen.

"Jake?" Brianna asked. "Do you want to see me dance? Chloe has a dance place—like the one my mom used to work at. And she taught me how."

Jake's brow arched of its own accord, as he glanced at sexy Chloe, imagining her doing a pole dance and ready to take her to task for teaching Brianna anything.

"Do you?" Brianna asked.

Did he what? "Excuse me?"

"Want to see me dance?"

"Okay." He wasn't sure what to expect, but the child psychologist was going to hear all about it at Brianna's next appointment. Jake would take him aside and…

"You two wait here," Brianna said before dashing off.

Jake rested his elbows on the table and stared at Chloe. "I wish you hadn't done that."

"Done what?"

He blew out a ragged breath. "I realize you and Desiree were friends. And that she seemed to think you were a whole lot like her—"

Chloe leaned forward, placing her own elbows on the table and causing her breasts to press forward, taunting him to react not only defensively, but hormonally, as well. "And *I* realize that you never liked Desiree and that you have no intention of giving me any more of a chance than you did her."

He couldn't argue with that.

She leaned back in her seat and tapped her nails—pink acrylic—on the table. "You ought to be far more concerned about the bad manners and the snobbish attitude your sweet little sister will learn from *you*."

Before Jake could decide whether he wanted to apologize or object, Brianna ran into the dining room wearing a lime-green tutu and a bright-eyed grin.

"Are you ready?" she asked.

"Yes." And a bit surprised to see her in a cutesy little outfit any other four-year-old girl might wear to a Saturday morning dance class at the YMCA.

Jake wasn't a ballet enthusiast by any means, but he watched Brianna attempt to mimic the graceful moves of a budding ballerina.

Okay. So he'd been wrong. Obviously, Chloe hadn't taught her anything seductive or inappropriate.

He wrestled with an apology for his speculation.

"I'm still learning all the steps, but when Chloe and me go to Bayside, I get to take lessons at her dance place. And I get to be in a recital with the other girls and wear pretty costumes like this one." Brianna glanced down at her tutu and fingered the ruffled edge.

Bayside, huh? No way. Brianna was going to stay in Texas with Jake.

The apology he'd been tossing around dissipated in a swirl of frustration buzzing overhead.

"They give dance lessons in Dallas, too," he said.

"You know what?" Brianna asked. "I'm going to show Mrs. Davies and Sweetie Pie what I can do." Then she skipped toward the kitchen.

"For what it's worth," Chloe said, "you've made a lot of false assumptions about me."

"Can you blame me?"

"As a matter of fact, I can." She stood. "But that's quite all right. I'm used to it."

The urge to apologize returned—stronger than ever. Jake seldom gave a rat's ass about what people thought of him, but it seemed to matter now. "I'm sorry, Chloe. It's just that Brianna said her mother used to work at a 'dance place,' so I figured—"

"You figured wrong. I own and operate a children's dance studio. Nothing fancy. Just a hole-in-the-wall place in the inner city. Perhaps you wanted me to make a distinction between that and the topless bar where her mother once worked, but I didn't see a reason to."

"No, Brianna doesn't need to know that."

Chloe crossed her arms. "For what it's worth, my dad won Eddie's Bar and Strip Club in a poker game.

And I was practically raised in an apartment upstairs. The girls who used to work for him as dancers and cocktail waitresses were very good to me. But I never had any idea what went on downstairs until I neared my teen years." She sat a bit straighter and lifted her chin, eyes flashing with determination and a strength Jake hadn't realized she had. "It's a part of my past and my reality. I won't downplay it, either. Nor will I allow you to suggest I should feel ashamed. I was loved and cared for as a child. Case closed."

"Again," he said, "I apologize."

She stared at him for a while, as though she wasn't sure whether to forgive him or not. "For the record, there were a lot of false assumptions you made about Desiree, too. And even though it's apparent she was sleazy in your eyes, she never, ever bad-mouthed you. Not in the sense that she believed you were a worthless piece of crap. She always said you would eventually come around and give her a chance. But unlike Desiree, I'm not convinced you would have, even if she'd lived to be one hundred."

The phone rang.

Glad for a reprieve, Jake answered. "Hello?"

A man introduced himself as Joe Davenport. "Is Chloe available?"

"Yes, she is." Jake passed her the phone.

"Hey, Joe!" Her voice lit up. Her eyes, too. Something warm cast a sweet spell on her face, wiping away the anger and sass. "It's *so* good to hear your voice. I miss you."

Her lover? Jake wondered. He reached for his nearly empty glass of iced tea, hoping she didn't think he was eavesdropping, which is just what he was doing. He wanted—no, make that *needed*—to glean more information about her, about her background. He might have misjudged her a bit, but he still didn't know squat about her.

"I sure appreciate that, Joe. Miss Priss never eats for the first few days after I'm gone. The vet says she tries to punish me for leaving." She reached for a curl at the side of her ear, then twirled it around her finger. "I should have brought her with me, but she's gotten so persnickety lately. I may need to fly back to California in a couple of weeks to attend a planning department meeting, so maybe I'll bring her back to Texas with me then. Flo and Ernie have been looking out for her, but I'm sure she's missing me."

Jake's first thought was that Chloe must have a cat. And that she planned to bring it to the ranch and turn it loose. Of course, that meant it would probably raise hell with the dog.

Great, all they needed was more friction. The ranch was buzzing with it already.

Then curiosity got the better of him. Why did she have a meeting with the planning department?

She laughed, a throaty chuckle that made him wish he'd been in on the joke. "How are my old folks?"

Her parents? he wondered.

"I expected as much." She blew out a sigh. "Mr.

Sickles wasn't at all happy about someone else taking over for me for a few weeks. And I'm a bit worried about him. He won't eat unless I sit and chat with him."

Another cat?

Chloe and Joe chatted on the phone for a while, then the call ended.

"Who was that?" Jake asked, in spite of himself. The caller had introduced himself as Joe, but Jake wasn't looking for a name. He wanted to know who the guy was and how he fit in.

"Joe's a friend."

Okay. But since the sound of "Joe's" voice had hit a light switch in Chloe's expression and turned her eyes a brilliant shade of green, a friend *and* lover seemed more likely. "Does he live with you?"

"No. He has a wife." She leaned forward and rested her elbows on the table. "Don't you have something better to do?"

"Not at the moment."

She opened her mouth to say something, then clamped it shut. Did she feel put on the spot? Guilty?

The married men Jake knew didn't claim single women, particularly the sexy variety like Chloe, as friends. So what was really going on?

And did Mrs. Joe know about it?

Chloe stacked the rest of the dishes that remained on the table, then lifted them. "I'd better help Mrs. Davies in the kitchen so that I can take a shower, fix myself a glass of warm milk and go to bed."

Jake glanced at his watch. It was only a little after

seven. She was definitely uneasy with his questioning. And he hadn't even gotten to the part about him laying down the ground rules.

"I didn't get much sleep last night," she added.

That made two nights in a row. He wondered if Brianna had kept her awake. If so, Jake had dropped the ball again. Maybe he ought to keep an ear peeled for his sister during the night so no one else had to.

He'd just settled into the reclining chair in the family room and begun to surf channels to find a show that interested him, when Chloe brought Brianna in to say good-night. The child wore a blue nightgown bearing a picture of Cinderella on the front.

Okay, so Chloe had been right about the princess thing. He'd keep that in mind from now on.

When Jake opened his arms, Brianna gave him a hug that nearly squeezed the heart right out of him. "Good night, Jake."

"Sleep tight, princess."

She broke out in a big grin. "You never called me that before."

"You're turning into one before my very eyes." Jake cupped her cheek. "So I'll make sure no one puts a pea under your mattress."

"Why would someone pee on my bed?" She cocked her head to the side.

"I'm talking about a different kind of pea. The kind you eat. And I was referring to a story someone read to me a long time ago."

"Mrs. Davies is going to read to me tonight," the little girl told him.

"That's good." Tomorrow Jake would volunteer to read to her. And actually, if truth be told, he was looking forward to it.

In the morning he would be leaving the ranch early. There was a board meeting in Dallas he'd tried to postpone, but hadn't been able to. While in town, he would stop by a bookstore or go to the library. *The Princess and the Pea*, if he could find it, would make a nice surprise. Better yet, maybe he'd also go shopping and buy her a toy that had something to do with castles and fairy tales.

After Brianna trotted off to bed, Chloe went to the kitchen and returned with a glass of milk.

"I thought you were kidding," he said.

"Excuse me?"

"About the warm milk."

"It seems to work, so I'll do whatever it takes."

"Insomnia?" he asked.

"It's a problem sometimes." She shrugged. "I don't sleep very well in strange surroundings or in different beds."

Thoughts of Chloe in bed, those that were familiar to her and those that weren't, made him ponder all kinds of reasons why she'd stay awake. And none of them had to do with the mattress.

She didn't say any more, and he didn't press.

"You know…" she said, yawning again and stretching like a cat in the sun. "I'm sorry, but you'll have to excuse me. I'm winding down and had better take advantage of it."

As she turned and padded down the hall, her hips drew his focus like the swaying coin dangling from a hypnotist's chain. Back and forth, side to side.

Damn, she had a sexy walk. The kind that made a guy consider following her....

Or taking a cold shower.

There was another option, though. One Jake might actually consider.

Maybe he ought to put on a pot of coffee and pull an all-nighter and get some extra work done. Besides, he didn't like the idea of Chloe prowling around the house while he was asleep.

And if she woke up tonight, he'd be waiting for her.

Chapter Five

The house was quiet, except for the incessant tick-tock from the clock on the mantel. The last time Jake had checked the time, it was well after two o'clock, and he pondered turning in for the night.

He was just about to climb from his seat on the brown leather recliner, when he heard the sound of feet padding down the hall.

The steps seemed to be too heavy for Brianna, and since Mrs. Davies had retreated to her room in the guesthouse located next to the outbuildings, he figured it had to be Chloe.

And he'd been right.

She entered the family room wearing a black tank shirt and a pair of blue-plaid boxer shorts. Her legs,

Miss-America long, were more shapely than he'd imagined—a remarkable asset he passed off to good genes and exercise.

"Are you still awake?" she asked.

"Yeah. I was just thinking about going to bed, though." He nodded his chin toward her. "I see the warm milk didn't help."

She glanced at his empty mug on the lamp table. "What were you drinking? Coffee?"

"I *was*. Do you want me to make another pot?"

"Not for me." She yawned, then took a seat on the sofa, drawing up those beauty-pageant legs and tucking her feet next to her bottom.

So much for going to bed now—at least, by himself. Sleep was the last thing on his mind.

On the other hand, sex was taking the lead. Not that he'd lose his head over Chloe. He knew better than that. Look what had happened to his old man on that Alaskan cruise ship.

But if Jake could keep his feet on solid ground, his testosterone in check and his mind on business, he just might get the chance to quiz her tonight, after all. To find out what—or rather, *who*—he was up against. Under normal circumstances, he prided himself at being able to sweet-talk information out of most people, but he and Chloe hadn't started off on the right foot.

Okay, so some of that had been his fault. He would need to watch his step from here on out. Another confrontation wouldn't do him any good. Instead, he'd have to use a let's-start-over-and-be-friends approach.

"So you own a dance studio," he said. "Tell me about it."

"There's not much to tell."

"Why'd you decide to open it?"

She paused for a moment, as though contemplating her answer. Or maybe trying to decide how much to share.

"It's a long story. Let's just say that I like kids and wanted to provide some of them a safe haven."

"I thought it was a dance studio."

"It is—so to speak. But it's a whole lot more than that. We're still in the baby stages, but I'm proud of what we've got so far."

He imagined she was. Owning a business was a dream for many people, one that was sometimes out of reach. "How long have you owned it?"

"About six months. Last summer I had an opportunity to buy a building in downtown Bayside, not far from the Rescue Mission, the Starlight Pool Hall and Eddie's. It had once been a five-and-dime store, but had been empty for years. Since it had been run-down and vacant for so long, it took me months to get it ready. I cleaned it out, put in new plumbing and electric wiring. Then I painted, replaced the flooring, that sort of thing." She grinned, then twirled a corkscrew curl around her index finger. "It looks good, if I do say so myself. It's the one bright spot on the street."

Jake sensed that she couldn't be doing too well financially. He could just imagine the kind of transients who might hang out in the area, so he suspected that the parents who could afford that sort of thing probably preferred a better—and *safer*—location. "How's it going? Are you making any money?"

"I didn't open the studio to make money."

Why the hell not? Who'd go to the expense of buying property, renovating an old building and opening a business without wanting it to be financially successful?

"I provide lessons for children who otherwise can't afford them, so I don't get much income. It's also become a local hangout for latchkey kids. Keeps them off the street." She shrugged again, then tossed him an unguarded grin. "I wouldn't expect you to understand."

Her response took him aback, and he wasn't sure what to say. What to think. It seemed…noble. And the fact she didn't think he'd understand made him… uneasy. As though she'd seen him as something less than he was.

"Were you a latchkey kid?" he asked, wondering if the place was an attempt to pay it forward.

"No, but I grew up in the inner city and have an appreciation for the people who are trying to eke out a life for themselves—both young and old. It's especially tough on the kids."

He had a feeling she had firsthand knowledge. "You mentioned living in the inner city. You didn't grow up on the streets, did you?"

"No. I had it pretty good in that regard."

"How so?"

She reached for the decorator pillow that adorned the sofa, plopped it into her lap and held it in front of her chest.

Cradling it?

Or shielding herself?

It was hard to say.

"I was born in Harbor Haven, a coastal town about thirty minutes north of San Diego. My folks never married, so I lived with my mom in a little cottage by the beach."

"When did you move to the inner city?"

"After my mom died." She shifted the pillow in her lap. "My dad was a gambler whose luck shifted from time to time. My mother loved him but had refused to marry him because she thought he was too irresponsible to take on a wife and baby. Ironically, she died when I was Brianna's age, so I ended up with my dad, anyway."

Her father, the gambler. Tough break.

"I'm sorry," Jake said.

"Don't be. Even though life was a bit unconventional, I never lacked for anything."

He sensed that wasn't true, but kept his mouth shut.

"About the time I came to live with my dad, he won the bar and strip club in a backstreet poker game. He saw Eddie's place as a way to settle down, to become a respectable business owner." She smiled wryly. "He may not have been Ward Cleaver or Dr.

Huxtable, but he loved me and had tried his best to give me everything a girl needed."

"Did he?" Jake asked. "Provide what you needed?"

Chloe shrugged. "No. There are some things money can't buy."

Jake opened his mouth to ask what those things were, but decided not to push too hard. She seemed to be opening up, telling him who she was, where she came from. "How'd you meet Desiree?"

"She worked for my dad."

"Dancing?"

"Not at first. And not at the end." Chloe shifted in her seat, yet held the pillow close. "Desiree had a lousy childhood. She'd never known her father, and her mom was an alcoholic who'd married and divorced three times. When Desiree was fifteen, one of her mom's boyfriends came on to her. She wasn't interested, but he insisted. She tried to fight him off, but he was too strong. When her mom came in, you'd have thought she would have torn the creep limb from limb. Instead, she blamed Desiree and beat the crap out of her. So Desiree left home that night, having decided that living on the streets was safer than being at home."

Damn. Jake hadn't given much thought to where Desiree had come from or why she'd made the choices she had. Apparently, her options had been limited.

"My dad found her panhandling in front of the bar one night and felt sorry for her. He'd offered her a job washing dishes and let her sleep in the storage room until she found another place to stay. When she turned eighteen and found out she could earn more money dancing, she'd asked one of the other girls to show her the ropes."

Chloe fingered the braided trim along the edge of the pillow she still held. "My dad spent a lot of time flying back and forth to Vegas, so the cocktail waitresses and the dancers who'd worked for him looked out for me. But Desiree and I had quickly bonded. There was only a ten-year age difference between us, and she became both a mother and big sister to me. She was also the best friend I ever had."

Jake wasn't convinced that Chloe's childhood was much better than Desiree's had been. That her upbringing had been any more respectable or stable.

Chloe cocked her head to the side. "By that splatter of skepticism on your face, I sense you're making value judgments again, and you're wrong."

Jake shrugged. "I'm sure Desiree was good to you."

"She was better than good." Chloe sat up straight and continued to clutch that damn pillow close to her chest. "I know what you're probably thinking, but you're wrong. Without any family support, she'd had to rely on her available resources—her beauty and her body. And as soon as she'd learned to tap into her brain, things began to look up for her."

Yeah. "And when she tapped into my dad on the cruise ship, things really changed." His words, which had rung true to him before, seemed a bit acerbic to him now, and he suspected they wouldn't sit right with Chloe.

He supposed he really couldn't blame Desiree for trying to move up and put the topless bar behind her, especially if his dad had been willing to marry her and bring her to Texas.

Chloe crossed arms. "In spite of what you think, Desiree never would have married your father for any reason other than love. So even though your theory falls neatly into your little box of assumptions, it's wrong."

"How can you be so sure?"

"Desiree always seemed to pick losers when it came to men, and for about five years, she'd sworn off dating, completely. Besides, by that time, thanks to her efforts, Eddie's was turning a decent profit and she'd urged my dad to sell the business and buy other properties, to diversify his holdings and investments. It worked out well for them both."

Jake's dad had always said that Desiree had brought her own money to the marriage, although Jake hadn't believed it. But maybe she had.

"How about you?" Chloe asked. "What was your childhood like?"

"It was all right."

Oh, yeah? an inner voice whispered. Sucky childhoods occurred on both sides of the tracks.

Jake wanted to brush off the past, but for some reason Chloe's honesty had struck a chord of intimacy between them, demanding he be just as open as she'd been.

"My dad met and married my mom after a whirlwind courtship, only to find months later that he'd made a big mistake. But by the time he'd come to that conclusion, I was on the way. They split right after I was born. My mom moved out and left me behind, and my dad had full custody during my early years."

Jake had been ten when he'd overheard his father discussing the details with a friend. His dad had offered his mom a bigger settlement in the divorce if she'd agreed to give him full custody of their infant son. It had hurt like the dickens to learn that his mother had sold him out, and Jake had slunk off to his room and cried that day. But he'd never mentioned his disappointment to either of his parents.

He'd continued to tell himself it hadn't been a big deal, and eventually he came to believe that was true.

"While you were growing up, did you spend any time with your mother?" she asked.

"Not at first. According to my dad, she had some airing out to do and didn't need the complications of having a baby in her life, which was probably the case. I didn't see very much of her until I started school."

"I'm sorry," she said. "I lost my mom and know how it feels to grow up without one."

It had been tough at times, although Jake didn't like admitting it. "It wasn't too bad. Once I got older, I started spending every other weekend with her, and our relationship developed over time. By the time I was in high school, I bounced back and forth between both houses in Dallas and the ranch. It might have been nice to have one place to really call home, but I never lacked any of the things money could buy."

Of course, his parents had often used money as carrots, so it hadn't taken long for Jake to realize that his mom and dad had been trying to buy his affection. He'd soon learned that money meant power and with it a man could have just about anything he wanted.

When his mom had insisted he would get a better education at an elite and private school in Dallas, she'd encouraged his dad to do whatever it took to get him accepted. Jake had never been sure what it had cost to get the school to find room for him, but he'd started third grade there in the fall. And the entire student body had seemed to be very happy about the new gym an anonymous benefactor had provided.

There was a downside to having money, though. Sometimes it attracted the wrong people, the ones who could be bought.

When Jake was in college and had been dating Susan Ellings, an attractive young woman of modest means, she'd sent an e-mail to a friend, who forwarded it to someone else. Somehow, it had landed in his in-box.

Susan's message to a sorority sister clearly implied that she was more interested in the Braddock family finances than she had been in Jake as a person. Needless to say, he'd ended things quickly. From that day on, he kept his heart out of his relationships.

"Are you close to your mom?" Chloe asked, drawing him out of the past.

"I try to be." His mom wasn't always an easy person to be close to.

Jake glanced at Chloe, watched her stretch, then cover her mouth with her fingertips and draw out a slow, sexy yawn.

She hadn't gone into great detail about herself, yet she'd seemed to be open and up front. In a way she was a contradiction—an innocent seductress, a gullible charmer.

But who was she, *really?* he wondered.

He couldn't help being intrigued by the sight of her curled up on the sofa, her hair tousled by sleep. She looked as though she belonged in bed.

A man's bed.

His bed.

Damn. He wouldn't go *there.* He kept his relationships shallow and noncommittal, but that didn't mean he would date a woman who wasn't respectable or conservative.

Chloe was no doubt a firecracker in bed, but she'd turn his life on end before the last wave of passion ended. And even though he preferred a no-strings-attached relationship, he still liked attending an occasional party or social function with a lady on his arm. One who caused a warm buzz of interest rather than a jaw-dropping, wide-eyed gape.

It was getting late; he was getting tired. His brain was slipping and his libido was busting to the forefront.

But not for long. It was time for a shower. A long, cold one.

And it was time to go to bed.

Alone.

Jake had gone over his calendar carefully and had postponed as many meetings and appointments as he could during the next six weeks, since he was stuck at the ranch. But today's Braddock Enterprises board meeting had been too important to put off. So even though a storm had loomed on the horizon, he'd made the hour-long trip to Dallas.

He might have made it home without being caught in the blinding rain, if he hadn't stopped at the bookstore across from the office, where he'd found *The Princess and the Pea* as part of an anthology of fairy tales. Or if he hadn't been sidetracked at the toy store, where he'd purchased a miniature castle and an assortment of royal characters Brianna could move around from the open-sided plastic structure. By the time they'd added up all the little extras, it had cost a pretty penny, but if it made her happy, he didn't care.

Now he had to face the consequences of the time spent in Dallas, as he headed back to the ranch, the windshield wipers swishing back and forth in high gear.

He ought to be sitting in the comfort of his luxury townhome, with Mrs. Davies looking after his sister there. Instead, he'd been driving for an hour in the pounding rain, which made him swear under his breath.

Aw, Desiree. What did I ever do to deserve this? Brianna would have done just as well in the city. I could have taken Mrs. Davies with me to look after her when I worked. And why did you throw Chloe into the mix....

Why couldn't she have stayed in Bayside where she belonged?

He parked his SUV near the barn, then grabbed the book and pulled out the box that held the ornate plastic castle and the shopping bag with a ton of other princess toys. Then he hurried through the rain to the back porch, where he took off his hat and wiped the mud from his boots.

Through the doorway into the kitchen, he spotted Mrs. Davies standing over the stove, where a pot simmered. The aroma of tomatoes, fresh green chili and cilantro filled the air. He wasn't sure what she was preparing for dinner, but it sure smelled good.

The dog, Sweetie Pie, snoozed on a pad in the corner by the stove.

"Where's Brianna?" he asked, depositing his packages on the kitchen table.

"In the living room, playing with Chloe." The older woman clucked her tongue. "It beats anything I ever did see. You'd think that woman was a kid herself."

"What are they doing?"

"I haven't got a clue, but the living room looks like a twister set down in the midst of it and the dog gave up trying to keep up with them about ten minutes ago."

Jake had half a notion to stomp into the other room and ask if Chloe had gone off the deep end. He wondered if Mrs. Davies would agree. There was only one way to find out. He'd hang out in the kitchen and quiz her. Something told him the woman had her opinion, and he suspected it matched his own.

When push came to shove and a custody decision was made, he was going to need someone in his corner.

He wasn't particularly thirsty, but he reached for a glass from the cupboard, anyway.

"There's lemonade in the fridge," Mrs. Davies said, "and I've got a pot of sun tea on the counter."

"Thanks." He opted for the lemonade, then took a seat at the table, intending to question the housekeeper, to see what her take was on this crazy situation. "How long have you known Chloe?"

"I met her last Friday morning when she left Brianna with me at the hotel and went to meet the attorney."

Jake took a long, steady drink of what he'd just realized was fresh-squeezed lemonade—no wonder his dad had hired the woman and Desiree had contracted her to stay on for a couple of years. Mrs. Davies went above and beyond in the kitchen.

"What do you think about Chloe?" he asked.

Mrs. Davies didn't answer right away. "Well, she's a bit…unorthodox."

To say the least.

"And if you ask me," the older woman said, "her wardrobe is R-rated most of the time."

Boy howdy.

Mrs. Davies turned and faced Jake, crossing her arms. "However, she's very nice, and Brianna likes her."

That part was good. But Chloe wasn't the least bit motherly. And Jake ought to know. He'd been checking out mothering styles for years, a habit he'd picked up when he'd been a little boy who hadn't had his mom around often enough.

When he finished his drink, he rinsed the glass and left it in the sink. Then he headed for the living room, bracing himself for a mess but still unprepared for a disaster.

Mrs. Davies hadn't been exaggerating. The furniture had been moved into an obstacle course, along with dining-room chairs, some of which had been turned upside down. Sheets and blankets had been tented over them, creating an indoor playground of sorts.

"What in blazes is going on in here?" Jake asked.

Brianna, a smile plastered on her bright-eyed face, crawled out from under the coffee table that had been draped with a beach towel. "We can't go outside because it's raining, so we made a fort instead. Want to climb in here and play with us?"

"I'll pass," he said.

Chloe's face peered out from a gap where the edge of a blue blanket met a yellow-striped sheet. "That's because you're a stick-in-the-mud."

For some dumb reason, he felt the need to bend, to get on his hands and knees and prove he knew how to have fun. He also felt compelled to defend his honor and that of all the other muddy sticks in the world. But Jake didn't play. Not like that. And his conservative habits, ingrained during his teen years, were hard to shake.

"Betcha can't find me," Brianna said, before dashing off on all fours.

Chloe gave a little shrug at Jake, her lips quirking in a bright-eyed smile of her own. "I bet I can."

As she turned and crawled away, a piece of sheet slipped, causing a breach in the fort and allowing him a glimpse of Chloe's denim-clad rear.

And what a shapely rear it was.

Brianna squealed, and Chloe giggled. Moments later the blue blanket fell away and the fort collapsed upon itself.

"Uh-oh," his little sister said. "We have to build it all up again."

"Actually," Chloe said, getting to her feet, "it'll be time for dinner soon. Why don't we put things back where they belong?"

"Good idea," Jake said. To be honest, he'd wondered if Chloe was going to leave the mess for the housekeeper. It was nice to know that she wouldn't.

"Oh, no." Brianna scanned the disheveled room. "Where's Sweetie Pie? He was here just a little bit ago, but now he's lost."

"He's in the kitchen," Jake told her.

"Can I go and make sure?" she asked.

"Go ahead," Chloe said, and the child dashed off.

"Shouldn't you make her stay here and help you put the room back in order?" It's what Jake's mother would have insisted upon if he'd gotten a wild hair and made a mess like this.

"Probably." Chloe placed her hands on her hips and scanned the upturned furniture and the sheet-and-blanket-littered floors. "But I'm afraid I was the one responsible for the bulk of this mess, and she's not big enough or strong enough to do much, anyway."

"Then I'll help you." Jake wasn't sure why he offered; he certainly hadn't turned the living room into a disaster zone. But when Chloe flashed him an appreciative smile, his pulse kicked up a notch, making him glad he'd volunteered.

Within minutes they had dining room chairs returned to their rightful place around the table, as well as the sofa cushions and other furniture put back where they belonged.

Chloe picked up two corners of the blue blanket. "Can you grab the other end?"

Jake did as she asked, then proceeded to match the edges, cooperating to get the task done. As their fingers brushed, their gazes locked. Their hands, too.

Time seemed to stand still, yet something shot between them, something warm and energizing. His pulse reeled and his blood surged.

He tore his gaze away and bent to pick up the bottom part of the blanket, hoping to break the brief connection.

As he brought up the corners to match the ones she

held, he was careful not to let his touch linger on her fingers, yet that little "something" continued to sizzle between them, piquing his interest, his attention.

It's just male hormones, he told himself. A natural reaction to a sexy woman's touch.

But Chloe appeared to be just as shaken by it as he'd been.

He'd be damned if he knew exactly what it was, though.

Or what he would do about it.

Chapter Six

As Chloe took the edge of the blanket from Jake, folding it into quarters, then eighths, their fingers touched and lingered.

The moment their eyes met, an unexpected surge of heat jolted her senses to life. She suspected he felt it, too, because she couldn't be the only one who sensed the hormones buzzing between them, the breath-stealing sexual awareness.

For one pulse-soaring moment, Chloe's heart and all she held dear lay naked before him.

She gripped the satin-wrapped edge of the material as though the partially folded blanket could hide her. All the while, she tried her best to shake off the intensity of his gaze and the thrum of her pulse.

Normally, she was careful who she agreed to date, who she allowed into her world. She chose men who were charismatic, bold and strong. Men who wouldn't be threatened by who she was, where she'd grown up. The last guy she'd dated had been Carlos Ramon, a suave Latin heartthrob she'd thought was "the one."

Her Spanish was limited, which had made their few dates unique and fun—until he'd proudly announced that he was a matador. She hadn't understood the entire conversation they'd been fumbling and grinning through, but she knew enough of the language to realize Carlos was a bullfighter.

Disappointment had risen in her ears like the roar of a crowd in a Mexican arena, and her hope for a relationship with a handsome Latin lover shattered.

Bulls could be mean, nasty brutes, but there was a beauty about them.

Carlos, with his equally limited English, had assumed she was an avowed animal lover, but it had been more than that. Chloe was a champion for the underdogs and the downtrodden—whether they had four legs or two. And she hadn't been able to find anything noble about a sport that brought an animal to its knees.

She'd taken a cab home that night—*alone*—and hadn't dated since. It's not as though she'd sworn off men, like Desiree had once done, but she'd decided to quit looking for a guy who would complete her life.

One way or another, each man she'd ever dated had let her down, and she'd come to believe she'd be more apt to find a leprechaun toting a pot of gold than the elusive soul mate she'd hoped was out there somewhere.

So what was with this sudden sexual attraction to Jake Braddock? A man *so* not her match?

The Texas businessman, with his stuffy ways and his uppity manner, wasn't the kind of man who normally stirred her interest or sent her pulse soaring. So why now? Why here?

"What's for dinner?" he asked, as though nothing had sparked between them.

"I'm not sure." She tried to force her focus on food, on the upcoming meal, but there was another hunger brewing. One she wasn't at all happy to admit.

"Something Mexican, I'll bet." Jake straightened the coffee table, making sure it sat square in front of the leather sofa. "That sauce sure smells good, doesn't it?"

So did the scent of his cologne, the smell of man and musk and rain, but she managed a nod.

Jake picked up a sofa cushion and shoved it into place. "I'm starving, how about you?"

The aroma from dinner had certainly stirred her appetite, but the craving for food paled next to the desire for more of Jake's touch. She did her best to ignore the emotions and urges brewing in her chest, hoping to get through dinner with her pride in check.

For years, Chloe had wanted to find a mate who

was a lot like her, a man who was honest and who had a heart for the less fortunate. And it was obvious Jake Braddock wasn't even in the running.

As they placed the last cushion on the chair and returned the lamps to the tables, Mrs. Davies called them to dinner. Jake shot Chloe one last glance, which set off a flurry of pheromones all over again.

Why the budding desire for a man who made no secret of his plan to take full custody of Brianna?

She tried to shrug off her stray thoughts and feelings all the way to the dining room, where they sat down to another delicious meal. As they ate their fill of cheese enchiladas, Spanish rice, refried beans and some kind of Mexican coleslaw that was out of this world, Chloe tried to keep up with the casual chatter and not appear the least bit affected by the man seated across from her.

"Guess what we're having for dessert?" Brianna asked.

"I don't have a clue." Jake placed his napkin on his plate. "But if it's anything like last night, I'm sure it'll be great."

"We're having some mores," Brianna said.

"Some more what?" Jake asked.

Chloe couldn't help but grin and realized she'd better explain. "She's talking about s'mores. It's a campsite goodie. So even though we had to put our fort away, we're going to wrap up the evening as if we were still out in the wilderness."

"And we get to have hot cocoa, too," Brianna added.

"We'll need your help, though." Chloe glanced at Jake, wondering if he'd play along.

He stiffened a bit, his stuffy nature apparently taking over. "What kind of help do you want?"

"Can you start a fire in the hearth?" she asked.

"It's *summer*," Jake said. "And even though it's been raining outside, it's hot and muggy. We'd have to really crank up the air-conditioning if we start a fire."

Chloe held up her hand and made the sign of a pinch. "We just need a little one. Just enough to melt a couple of marshmallows and some chocolate."

Jake seemed to wrestle with her request. She suspected he might have eventually weakened, anyway, given a moment or two longer, but the minute Brianna threw out a "pretty please," he was toast.

While Mrs. Davies shooed them out of the dining room and insisted she could handle cleaning up the dishes alone, they went into the family room.

"I can't believe I'm doing this." Jake stooped before the hearth and began to light the gas logs.

"We appreciate your help," Chloe said. "While you get the fire going, Brianna and I will get the ingredients we'll need. But don't go anywhere. We'll be back in a minute."

The dog followed them to the kitchen.

Mrs. Davies, who was waiting for the sink to fill with warm, soapy water, turned and smiled. "Why don't I feed Sweetie Pie so he won't try to mooch all the s'mores?"

"Good idea," Chloe said.

After she'd gathered graham crackers, Hershey bars and marshmallows, they returned to the family room with the simple ingredients on a platter.

Earlier today, while looking for TV trays to extend their tented fort, Chloe had found a couple of empty wire hangers in the coat closet in the entry, so she retrieved those, as well.

Before long they were seated Indian-style before the flame.

"This is going to be so much fun," Brianna said. "I never got to go camping before."

"I never knew you wanted to." Jake placed a hand on her small shoulder. "We'll have to take you on a real camping trip some day."

We'll have to take you?

The way he'd said it made Chloe wonder whether the two of them had become some kind of parental team and might actually take Brianna on outings together.

She handed a coat hanger to Jake. "Will you help me straighten one of these?"

"I can't believe you roped me into this." Still, he unwrapped the edges of the wire and worked to make it straight.

Chloe laughed. "Think of this as an exercise in character building."

"Oh, yeah?" Jake chuckled, a soft yet gravelly sound that stroked her senses. "You sound like my dad. And for the record, my character doesn't need building."

Actually, she could see a lot of room for improvement, although she wasn't sure he'd agree. A grin tickled her lips. "It wouldn't hurt you to be more flexible. And a bit more spontaneous."

He grumbled under his breath, and another grin tugged at her lips. "You're as stiff and rigid as the coat hanger you're working on."

"I'm not either."

Her grin deepened, but she kept quiet.

When the first marshmallow was a golden brown and began to droop from the wire, Chloe sandwiched it between two graham cracker halves and a square of milk chocolate. Next, she broke off a piece and offered it to Brianna. "Try a bite of this, Breezy."

"Yum," the girl said. "You should eat some, Jake."

Chloe broke off a second piece and handed it to him. Their eyes met, and she thought for a moment he would reach for what she'd offered him.

He didn't, though.

So she forced the issue and lifted it to his mouth. "Open up."

He did as she instructed, and she placed the gooey goodie in his mouth. As her fingers brushed his lips, their gazes locked. Whatever had sparked between them before did so again, only stronger, more insistent, sucking her into a romantic fantasyland, where they lay on a heart-shaped mattress and fed each other chocolate-covered strawberries and whipped cream.

How crazy was that?

She tore her gaze from his and blew out a silent, "Whew."

It was getting warm in here, and the fire in the hearth didn't have anything to do with it.

She tried her best to ignore the heat, to pretend that Jake hadn't caused her world to shift in the wrong direction.

They made several more of the chocolaty treats. All the while, Chloe clung to the silence. Yet she couldn't ignore the stir of her senses, the focus on the handsome man sitting beside her. If she moved just a tad, if she shifted ever so slightly to the right, her knee would touch his.

"Can I take a little piece to Sweetie Pie," Brianna asked, "just so he can have a taste?"

"Chocolate isn't good for dogs." Jake turned to Chloe as though seeking her opinion. Or maybe her support.

"He's right. But why don't you ask Mrs. Davies to give you a small piece of graham cracker for him."

When Brianna dashed off, Jake shook his head. "That can't be a whole lot better."

"But it shouldn't hurt. Besides, she wants to share something with Sweetie Pie."

"If that dog gets the fox trots after eating sweets, you're going to be the one taking her outside all night long—*not me.*"

"I like to live dangerously," she said.

"I can see that."

Could he?

Their eyes met, and she wondered what he "saw." Could he peer into the naked heart of her? Was he aware of the hopes and dreams she harbored? Or the disappointments she'd suffered?

Jake turned back and glanced at the fire, watched the flames lick the artificial log.

"You ought to loosen up more often," Chloe said. "Sitting cross-legged on the floor suits you."

"Oh, yeah?" A grin tweaked his mouth and crinkled his eyes, but he continued to stare ahead.

"Were you ever a Boy Scout?" she asked.

"Nope. Between sports and my studies, I didn't have much time for that sort of thing."

"That's too bad." Desiree had gone out of her way to make sure that Chloe was able to balance her schoolwork with fun.

"How about you?" Jake asked. "You seem to have a knack for this sort of thing, which makes me think you were big on camping and scouting, yourself, as a kid."

"I would have liked to have been." Chloe paused for a moment, pondering her words. "When I was in junior high, a group calling themselves the Wilderness Girls started up at my school, but when I tried to join, the troop leader told my dad that they'd already reached their maximum number of members."

She'd been disappointed, of course, but she'd understood.

Then, a week later, Chloe learned that two other girls had been admitted. It had hurt to be shunned, but she couldn't see any point in mentioning it to Jake. He would never understand what it was like wanting to fit in. He might, however, benefit from knowing how special his stepmother had been, how kindhearted and loving.

"Desiree knew how badly I'd wanted a camping experience, so she planned an outing in the mountains near Julian. And I've got to tell you, I always appreciated how much that trip cost her."

"Where'd she take you? On some kind of private, guided excursion or something?"

"No, it was just the two of us. And when I said cost, I wasn't talking about money. If you knew Desiree, at all, you'd know she was a real girlie girl. She wasn't big on the outdoors, dirt or mosquitoes, so the weekend was brutal on her."

It hadn't been the first time Desiree had come up with a way to soothe the girl's feelings, to find an alternative plan. Even if it required self-sacrifice.

"Desiree went to the limit," Chloe said, "and never complained. Not even about the cold-water showers, the shortage of toilet paper, the camp food. She did, however, gripe about the poison oak she managed to get in places I won't mention."

Jake chuckled. "I got it once, and that stuff can be nasty."

"Poor Desiree. She smelled of calamine lotion for days." Chloe tossed Jake a pretty smile.

He couldn't help noticing she'd worn off her lipstick during her romp through the makeshift tents and all through dinner. Her makeup had faded, too, revealing a scattering of girlish freckles across her nose.

She'd mentioned that she thought he needed to let loose more often, but she ought to, too. When she dropped that sexy facade, she was far more attractive, more arousing.

There was a down-home way about her that was downright appealing. He reached out and touched a corkscrew strand of hair, letting it twist around his finger. "Pretty color."

"Thank you."

"Is it natural?" He didn't know why he asked. Maybe because there was a lot about her that didn't seem real. Women could buy just about anything these days.

"Yes, it's the real McCoy. I colored it black once, but Desiree came unglued. She told me that my red hair was my prettiest asset and that I was crazy to try and hide it."

For once he agreed with Desiree.

Realizing he still held on to Chloe's hair, he let it go, watched the tendril spring back to where it belonged—wild and free.

His gaze slid to her face. Her eyes glistened and her lips parted. Before his good sense deserted him completely, he turned back to the fireplace and tried to focus on the warmth that radiated from the artificial flames, rather than the heat that simmered between them.

It wasn't until Brianna returned with Sweetie Pie on her heels that he was able to shift his thoughts away from the sexy woman beside him.

But not too far.

The fire in the hearth cast a cozy glow throughout the house, making it feel more like a home than it ever had before—something that left him uneasy.

His dad had always insisted he come to the ranch on weekends, that it would be good for him to experience the outdoors, that it would help make a better man out of him. But Jake had never felt comfortable here. Not that he'd been all that at ease in his mother's place, either.

Yet for some reason there was something appealing about this house now. Something fresh out of a Norman Rockwell painting.

Heck, even the ugly dog, with its fur shiny and clean and a bright-pink bow tied around its neck, seemed to be settling in for a long winter's nap.

And it was the beginning of summer.

Damn, it was getting warm in here. Jake ran a finger along the inside of his collar.

As Chloe and Brianna headed to the bathroom, where the child would bathe and get ready for bed, Jake turned off the fire and proceeded to kick up the air-conditioning another notch.

A moment later he heard footsteps and watched Chloe return carrying a scrunched tissue at arm's length and heading toward the front door.

"What are you doing?" Jake asked.

She continued on her trek, but managed to explain. "There was a spider in the tub. I'm taking him outside."

"Wouldn't it have been easier to flush it?"

"And *kill* it?" She looked at him as though he'd suggested she ought to place a litter of kittens into a gunny sack and toss the whole kit and caboodle into a raging river.

"It's just a spider," he reminded her.

"I know. And he belongs outdoors."

Jake slowly shook his head. He'd wanted to get to know the real Chloe, but there was a lot more to her than met the eye.

Is that why she spent so much time on her appearance? Why she wore bright colors and revealing clothes?

Was she trying to keep people, particularly men, from looking too deep?

If so, it made him all the more curious about her and about what she didn't want people to see.

The next morning, after breakfast, Chloe went into the office to access the Internet. She had a real-estate deal pending in South Bayside and was expecting an e-mail from her attorney, who'd wanted to change the language in the counteroffer they'd received.

Chloe tried to surround herself with professionals who could advise her, but at times like this, she really missed Desiree, who'd often pointed out observations and possibilities Chloe hadn't considered. Desiree had not only invested Chloe's father's holdings and encouraged him to diversify his interests, she'd also insisted Chloe go to the junior college and pick up some accounting and business classes.

"You'll never know when it might come in handy," she'd told Chloe.

And she'd been right.

About a year ago, when Chloe's father had died unexpectedly, Chloe had become the successor trustee of his properties and holdings. A few days after the funeral, Chloe had met with Desiree and discussed her options, then shared her ideas for the future. Desiree had thought she was on track, so Chloe had opted to sell everything, then reinvest in a respectable office building and put the rest in some money-market accounts.

So far everything had gone according to plan. Chloe was pretty much set financially and had no reason to work, other than to support the many charities she championed. Her primary focus these days was her studio downtown, where she provided free dance lessons for disadvantaged children, hoping to give them something their parents couldn't afford.

But this project hadn't been part of her original strategy. Assuming the deal to buy the Belmont Arms went through, it would be another purchase made from the heart, just as her dance studio had been.

As she signed in, the familiar computerized voice announced, "You've got mail."

Chloe skimmed her messages, finding one from Joe Davenport, her old neighbor. Joe and his wife, Kristin, had been looking after Chloe's condo while she was in Texas. And according to Joe, all was going well on the home front.

"Wow," Chloe said, as she read the paragraph that

announced the babies had taken their first steps. When Joe and Kristin had been blessed with twin daughters nearly twelve months ago, they'd moved from their condo in Chloe's complex to a bigger house near the bay. They already had an eight-year-old son, so they'd needed a bigger place.

From: Chloe
To: Joe
That's great news! I can't wait to see the girls toddling after Bobby.

The next e-mail was from Kay Logan, a woman Chloe had met while working at a Tijuana orphanage. Kay also served on the boards of several different charities Chloe supported. Coincidentally, Kay's husband, Harry Logan, a retired detective, was a close friend of Joe's. But Chloe had only recently learned that the men knew each other, too.

From: Kay
To: Chloe
Would you be willing to serve on a committee I'm heading?

Chloe wasn't big on participating in groups. Instead she preferred to give anonymous donations. Whenever she did work with others on a project, she was choosy about who she'd work with. But Kay was a very special lady, and Chloe had a lot of respect for her.

So did everyone else in the community. Kay Logan had recently been chosen Bayside Woman of the Year.

We're putting on a dinner and a show in the fall. The proceeds will benefit Casa de Paz.

That particular charity, a home for abused women, was one of Chloe's favorites, and she was touched that Kay had asked.

From: Chloe
To: Kay
I'd be happy to, but I'll be out of town for the next five weeks. Is there anything I can handle by telephone or by e-mail until I return?

She hit the send button, then scanned several e-newsletters—one from the Feline Rescue Society and one from Suppers for Shut-ins.

Next, she found the e-mail she'd been waiting for: The revised contract from her attorney, Ron Erickson.

The deal they were negotiating was the purchase of a cheap hotel in the inner city, not far from her dance studio. The Belmont Arms had once been a modest little brick hotel, but was now little more than a graffiti-covered flophouse. No one, including her attorney and her CPA, was entirely convinced the investment would bear fruit. But Chloe didn't care. Several of her old folks lived in the run-down building, and she'd been concerned about their living conditions and their safety.

Since she'd been making daily stops there as a volunteer for the Suppers for Shut-ins program, she was concerned for her own safety, too—as well as that of the other volunteers. If she owned the property, she would have more control over security issues.

From: Ron Erickson
To: Chloe
There's a planning department meeting next week. I realize you're out of town, but if you can make it, I would suggest you do so. Your efforts with the dance studio, and now this project, have caused some of the council members to take note of your philanthropic efforts, especially in light of the city's redevelopment plan.

Could it be happening? Chloe wondered. Could she finally be gaining the respect she'd always longed for? The legitimacy her father had tried unsuccessfully to buy with new clothes, nice cars and private schooling?

Hope wasn't something she allowed herself to stew in, though. There'd been too many times in the past when she'd been optimistic, then had been disappointed.

From: Chloe
To: Ron
I'll be at the meeting.

And she would, even if it meant taking Brianna with her.

Desiree would have understood, although Jake might put up a fight.

As Chloe continued to scan and respond to e-mails, an overwhelming sense of being watched settled over her. She didn't need to turn and look to see who was there. She could feel Jake's presence, sense his musky scent. Still, she looked, anyway, and spotted him in the doorway.

He leaned against the doorjamb, arms crossed. His expression was as intriguing as it was unreadable.

Unable to think of anything else to say, she uttered, "Hi, there."

"What are you doing?" he asked.

"Answering e-mail." She leaned back in the desk chair, the tufted leather and metal springs creaking.

He just stood there, looking sexy, and studied her.

So she studied him right back.

He looked especially good this morning. Usually, his dress, his expression, his demeanor, was that of a businessman. Yet today, looking totally relaxed and dressed in worn denim jeans and a black shirt, he'd slipped into rancher/cowboy mode.

It suited him.

Jake Braddock was an intriguing man and incredibly attractive. But she'd found that men like him only had one thing in mind when dating her. Not that the thought of sex wasn't crossing her mind at this very moment.

She suspected making love with him would be...

nice, but she knew better than to set herself up for disappointment. He'd try to mold her and make her into
something she wasn't, and her best would never be
good enough.

It hadn't taken more than her share of bruised
feelings and one broken heart for Chloe to learn
how to skim the wrong kind of men from her dating
pool. That was why many of her relationships didn't
last long. And why her pickings had become slimmer
and slimmer with each passing year.

Still, Jake was nice to look at.

Maybe even to dream about.

Unfortunately, the six-week stint at the ranch was
going to make things a bit…sticky if she didn't shake
the attraction to a man who'd make her life miserable.

Jake uncrossed his arms and entered the office. "I
suppose one of the things we ought to do is have the
books audited."

Chloe reached into the drawer and pulled out a
file, not missing his "we" reference but choosing
not to react to it. "Desiree had it done recently.
You'll find that she was pretty thorough in regards
to money and business."

A flash of doubt crossed his face, but he picked up
the file, glanced at the contents. As he did so, his focus
intensified, completely absorbing his skepticism.

Moments later he looked up. "Thellar and Ames
is a topnotch accounting firm."

"That doesn't surprise me in the least. Desiree
was meticulous in her records and in choosing pro-

fessional representation." Chloe spun her chair toward Jake, saw his furrowed brow. Apparently, he'd been surprised to learn that Desiree had dotted her *i*'s and crossed her *t*'s.

"I glanced over the report yesterday," Chloe admitted. "A person almost needs a master's degree in accounting to be able to read it, but it appears to be in order."

Jake nodded.

Through the pensive silence, the computerized voice announced, "You've got mail," notifying Chloe of a new message in her inbox.

Out of curiosity and habit, she tore her focus from Jake and glanced at the screen. When she recognized the return address, she gasped. "Oh, my God..."

"What's the matter?" Jake looked up from the file he'd been studying.

Chloe didn't need a mirror to know the color had drained from her face or an EKG to know her heart rate had shot off the chart.

"You look like you just saw a ghost," Jake said, an observation that didn't surprise Chloe one bit.

"In a way I have." She pointed to the screen.

It was an e-mail from Desiree.

Chapter Seven

An e-mail from Desiree?

Impossible, Jake thought. He'd gone to the funeral, seen her laid to rest. His stepmother was dead.

Wasn't she?

She'd requested a closed casket, though.

No, this was a joke. And even though he believed in an afterlife, he doubted the good Lord provided Internet access.

Jake slipped around the desk and stood behind Chloe's seat, scanning the screen. Sure enough, the date and time sent claimed it was a brand-new e-mail. And that it had been sent by Desiree—or, more likely, someone using her e-mail address.

Was it some kind of trick?

"What does it say?" he asked Chloe.

She reached for the mouse and clicked it open.

From: Desiree

To: Chloe

Dear Chloe,

I'm not sure where I'll be when you read this note, but I scheduled it to arrive three weeks before Brianna's birthday. It might be difficult for her to celebrate this year, so I've scheduled another message meant for the fourteenth of July. I'll leave it up to you to decide whether to share it with her or not.

You know, I never had reason to celebrate birthdays when I was growing up. But then I came to work at Eddie's and met everyone there. Remember Candy? The petite blonde who had an eye for your dad? She threw a surprise party for me one year, and I was so touched that I've always tried to celebrate the special days of others.

Remember that Thanksgiving Day when you were nine and I took you to help me serve dinner at the Rescue Mission? When you heard Brother James talk about God, you asked him about Heaven. Your mother had been gone for more than a year, and you wanted to know if she was happy there. James gave you some wonderful answers, and although I took them to heart, I wasn't sure you believed him.

I wish that I could truly send you a message from

Heaven, one in which I could tell you firsthand how beautiful it is, how peaceful and full of love.

Please believe that it's everything Brother James had said it would be. Believe it for me—and especially for Brianna.

It's my deepest wish that all is going well on the ranch, although I suspect there has been some tension. I know it's not Jake's favorite place to be, but he's a cowboy at heart, just as his father was. Gerald used to always say that Jake thrived outdoors and that given the chance, he'd make the ranch his home.

Either way, the time spent there will be good for both him and Brianna. And in the long run, it will be good for you, too. You've been working way too hard.

Well, I'm getting a little woozy from the medication, so I'd better go back and lie down. If we're allowed to make requests in Heaven, I'll ask God to send Brianna a cotton-candy day for her birthday.

Love, Desiree

Jake continued to stand over Chloe, breathing in her peaches-and-cream scent and trying to ignore it so he could deal with the issue at hand.

The note he'd just read had most certainly come from Desiree. Who else knew how much Jake's dad had wanted him to enjoy living here? Who else knew how much Jake preferred life in the city?

JUDY DUARTE   119

Instead of voicing these questions aloud, though, he asked, "What's a cotton-candy day?"

Chloe turned and smiled, tears streaming down her cheeks. "It's a day when the sky is a clear blue easel and the clouds are puffy and form pictures. When I was a little girl, Desiree would take me outdoors and we'd point out different things to each other, like sheep and castles and snowmen."

Jake raked a hand through his hair, a bit uneasy with Chloe's tears, with the memories she had of Desiree—motherly things he'd missed out on in his life.

Brianna and Chloe had lost a whole lot more, yet a subtle sense of loss hovered over him, and he'd be damned if he knew how to shake it.

He wished that back when he'd had the chance, he had taken time to get to know his stepmother, to see her the way his father had, the way Chloe did. Instead he'd clung to the image he'd created of her and, as a result, he'd wasted the only chance he had to reconsider.

"I'm sorry," he said.

Chloe nodded, as though she knew what he was apologizing for, when he wasn't entirely sure, himself.

"Desiree was a special lady," Chloe said, "and she taught me a lot."

"Like what?" he asked, surprised that the answer mattered, that he really wanted to know.

"It's not like there was one particular lesson, but for what it's worth, I've started a journal of the things I've learned from her over the years. Someday I'll share it with Brianna."

"What have you written so far?"

"Just simple things," she said. "Like always look your best. And never limit your options."

It sounded as though she was gathering sage quotes and pieces of advice. But did she have enough to fill a journal? He couldn't imagine she would.

"Probably one of the most important lessons I learned," Chloe said, "was that families don't have to be related by blood."

Obviously, that had been an easy conclusion for the two of them to come to, assuming they were as close as Chloe said they were.

Chloe turned her chair away from the computer screen. "Desiree had always wanted to be part of a family. I think that's why she tried so hard to be both a mother and sister to me."

"And why it was so important for her to draw me into the fold," Jake said, surprised he'd voiced the thought out loud. But the theory made sense—if he could believe what Chloe had told him.

"When Desiree found out she was expecting Brianna, she'd been thrilled and couldn't wait to call me and share her good news."

Desiree *had* been happy, Jake realized. So had his father. They'd wanted Jake to share their joy, but to be honest, it had been embarrassing for him. After all, Gerald Braddock had been in his sixties and Desiree had been young enough to be his daughter.

"You may not know this, but I'm Brianna's god-mother." Chloe laughed softly, the lilt of her voice taunting him with an innocent, girlish charm. "A couple of months ago, Desiree had brought Brianna to Bayside. I hadn't seen her since she was a baby. When we were introduced, Brianna had been in awe of me."

Jake wasn't sure why. Desiree had been every bit as colorful and flamboyant as Chloe could be.

"Do you know why?" Chloe's eyes glistened and her smile deepened. "Brianna thought she was being introduced to her *fairy* godmother. You know, the princess thing."

Now *that,* Jake could imagine.

"We told her I wasn't that kind of godmother, but I think she still believes I'm hiding a wand and my wings. And that I'll pull them out of a magical closet someday."

Jake grinned, but he wondered if the title of godmother was legit. "I didn't think Brianna had ever been christened."

"Oh, yes. She was. When she was a couple of months old."

Why hadn't Jake known about it? Didn't people, especially family members, get invited to stuff like that? "No one told me."

"That's probably because it didn't happen in Dallas."

Still, he should have been told and given the option to attend or not. "If it wasn't in Dallas, where was it?"

"It was held at the Rescue Mission in Bayside."

"Why there?" he asked.

"Desiree and Brother James sort of had a...well, I'm not sure what you'd call it. But it was important to her to have him be a part of it."

"They had a 'thing'?" Jake asked. "You mean she dated a preacher?"

"No. Desiree wasn't a churchgoer. She went once or twice but said the people seemed uppity and turned their noses up at her. But sometimes, late at night, she used to invite Brother James up to the apartment for coffee. Then they'd have these deep philosophical chats. You know how wealthy people have personal shoppers? Well, she used to consider James her personal pastor."

At Desiree's funeral, a long-haired preacher officiated. He'd worn Birkenstocks and frayed jeans with a hole in the knee. The guy had come up to Jake afterward and introduced himself as James Clearwater. He was friendly enough, but Jake figured he was a flake or a member of a cult or something. The religious leaders he knew all wore suits or robes or something that made them look spiritual.

"I don't suppose Brother James flew into Dallas for the funeral," Jake said.

"Yes, he did. He's a really nice guy. I hope you got a chance to meet him."

"I did." Jake had made sure he'd been paid the proper stipend, but he really hadn't wanted to converse with someone who'd seemed so...laid back...and...unorthodox.

Now he wished he had. He might have asked James about Desiree, about some of the talks they'd had.

Too bad he couldn't turn back the clock and do a lot of things differently.

"Was my dad at the christening?" Jake couldn't imagine his dad attending. Not at the Rescue Mission. He could, however, see his father standing proudly at the altar in a cathedral or even a white clapboard church with an old-fashioned steeple.

Instead, he figured his dad would have stayed in Dallas to work. Or if he'd gone to San Diego, that he'd gone golfing or stayed in the hotel room watching a ball game. That he'd humored his wife and found something else to do.

"Yes, Gerald was there. That was the first time I met him and the only time I'd seen him in person."

"What did he have to say about it?"

"If he had any qualms about it, he never complained."

"Was there anyone else from Texas in attendance?" Jake asked.

"No. It was just a small gathering." Chloe crossed her arms and slid him a crooked grin. "It sounds as though you regret having missed it."

No. Just that he'd not been told or invited. He shrugged. "I probably would have been too busy to fly to California, anyway."

"It's probably just as well that you didn't go. I'm sure you would have been out of your comfort zone."

"What do you mean by that?"

"Desiree gravitated toward the people who truly cared about her. That meant that some of her friends wouldn't have fit in with your crowd."

He suspected she was right.

"In fact, you probably would have thought they were misfits, but Desiree had always been able to look beyond the outer trappings."

"You mean because her friends work at a bar and strip club? I'd think Brother James would have more of a problem with them than I would have."

"Some of her former coworkers were there, too, but I was thinking about a homeless woman named Sadie who keeps her valuables in a shopping cart. And Lucky Lewellyn, a Vietnam vet who spins tall tales outside of Carla's Coffee Shop." She tucked a strand of hair behind her ear. "And as for Brother James? No problem. Those were the people he was trying to reach, the ones he ministers to."

"So those people—Sadie and Lucky—attended Brianna's christening?" Jake asked, still struggling with the fact that he'd been excluded.

"Yes, and a few others, too. In fact, after Desiree passed away, Brother James conducted a memorial service for her in Bayside—at the Rescue Mission. The place was packed, so needless to say I wasn't the only one who was blessed to have been her friend."

Jake had been related to Desiree for six years, yet he hadn't really known her. Hadn't ever wanted to. But he'd be damned if he'd admit it. "So how many lessons have you written down in that journal?"

"I've got about forty or fifty so far. I jot them down whenever they come to mind."

"So it's an ongoing project."

She nodded. "Just last week, when I received the call that she'd passed away, I learned two new lessons."

"What were they?"

"Life is precious and short," Chloe said. "And everything can change in the blink of an eye."

She had that right, but before he could respond, Brianna's voice sounded from the doorway. "Have you guys seen Sweetie Pie? We're playing hide-and-go-seek, and it's my turn to find him."

"Sorry, Breezy." Chloe stood. "He's not in here. But I have a question for you."

"What's that?"

"Your birthday is coming up, and I wondered if you'd like to have a party."

Jake watched his sister, saw a smile cross her face as she lifted a hand and showed him all of her fingers. "I'm going to be five."

"I *know*," Chloe said. "Do you want a party this year?"

"Every kid wants a party," Jake said. "I'll call my country club and reserve a room for the evening. We can have a dinner and you can be the guest of honor."

"What's that?" Brianna asked.

"The birthday girl," Jake explained.

"I'd rather be a princess."

Jake glanced first at the redhead, then at his little

sister. "You can dress like a little princess. We'll take you shopping and buy you a new dress and shoes."

Brianna brightened. "Can we have balloons and a birthday cake?"

"Of course. What's a party without cake and ice cream and balloons?" Chloe smiled, first at Jake, then at Brianna. "You can plan the party, Breezy. Just tell us what you want."

"Okay. But right now, I better go find Sweetie Pie before he thinks I forgot all about him."

As the girl dashed off, Jake headed for the phone. "I'll call the club and lock in the date."

"Maybe we ought to have the party here," Chloe said. "Children would be bored in a country-club setting."

"It's a nice place." Besides, that's where his mother had always planned his parties. She'd married into money, first with his dad and more recently with his stepfather, a respected anesthesiologist. But she knew social etiquette inside and out.

"We just gave Brianna permission to plan her own party," Chloe said.

"Actually, *you* gave her permission," Jake said, "But she can be involved in the planning."

Chloe folded her arms. "I'm going to give her free rein."

"Only to a point," Jake countered.

Chloe stood her ground, her crossed arms thrusting her breasts forward. Even when she wasn't trying, she had a sexy aura.

She wasn't wearing any makeup this morning, not that he could tell. And her hair had yet to be spritzed. The curls were relaxed in a soft tumble around her shoulders and down her back. There was a glimmer in her eyes and a fire in her soul that challenged him. Taunted him.

If things were…different…

If he'd met her while at a convention. Hell, if he could keep things shallow, he might…

Damn. Was he crazy? It was still morning, yet she had him wishing he could go back to bed again. And not alone.

The walls of the office closed in on him, and he decided to make a break for it.

A woman like Chloe might drive him wild in bed, but she'd also create havoc in his life.

Chloe hadn't seen Jake since shortly before noon. Now Brianna, who'd already bathed, was watching a cartoon movie in the family room with Mrs. Davies, Jake's dinner was on the stove and Chloe was standing on the porch, studying the sunset.

Okay, so a small part of her was waiting for him to return. She enjoyed their banter, even though it bordered on sparring sometimes. It kept her alert.

So far, she liked staying on the ranch, just as Desiree had said she would. There was a peace and tranquility found in the slower pace that downtown Bayside didn't offer. But for the most part, Chloe was a city girl. She loved the nightlife—the theater, ballet.

Yet when she stood outdoors at dusk, watched the sun sink low in the west, heard a horse whinny in the pasture, it made her long for something she'd never had. Something she hadn't realized was missing.

Not that it had been completely restful here. She had to stay on her toes around Jake, and they'd butt heads a couple of times already. She suspected there would be more confrontations in the future—Brianna's birthday party came to mind. But that didn't mean she wouldn't use the time here to unwind and to refill the well.

She rested her hands on the oak railing, awed by the way the sun had painted streaks of orange and pink in the sky.

How many times had Desiree stood in this very spot, filled her lungs with the same alfalfa-laced fresh air?

Footsteps sounded on the graveled walkway to the barn, and she turned to see Jake walking toward her. After taking his turn on the office computer this morning, he'd gone outside and talked at length to Ozzie Bedford, the ranch foreman. She'd expected him to return to the house, but instead she'd been told he had saddled one of the horses and taken off.

As he made his way to the porch, he carried himself with a long, lean cowboy swagger, something she hadn't noticed about him when he wore business apparel.

He hadn't made any secret of the fact that he didn't like ranch life, that he'd rather be in Dallas. Yet his father and Desiree had disagreed. In the years Chloe had known Desiree, she'd learned to respect her friend's ability to read into people—at least the ones she hadn't gotten romantically involved with.

"Hey," Chloe said, drawing herself up straight. "When you missed dinner, I thought about filing a missing persons report on you."

He lifted his Stetson and wiped the perspiration from his brow with the back of his hand. Then he shrugged. "I just felt the need to get away for a while."

"Did it help?"

He replaced the hat on his head, adjusting it as though he knew just how it ought to feel when it was on right. "Yep. As a matter of fact, it did. I may not like living out here, but I enjoy riding. And having time to think."

The ranch, she supposed, with its green rolling hills dotted with colorful patches of wildflowers, would provide a lot of time to ponder life, to reflect on the past and to consider the future. "Maybe I'll have to try it, myself."

He stepped onto the porch and closed the distance between them. "Do you know how to ride?"

"A little, but I'm not Dale Evans, if that's what you mean."

He opened his mouth, as though he might offer to remedy that, then clamped it shut.

She probably ought to let it go, but she'd always loved horses, ever since the summer before ninth grade, when she'd read *The Black Stallion, King of the Wind* and *My Friend Flicka*. It had been more than ten years, and the titles still came to mind.

Back then, she'd known it wasn't feasible to own a horse when they lived in the heart of the city, so she'd never mentioned it to her father. But when a couple of the Preston Prep girls claimed to have horses they boarded outside of Bayside on a ranch that also gave riding lessons, Chloe had begged her father to take her there and enroll her.

At first she'd been in heaven. But then her classmates, both of whom had been part of the Wilderness Girls, began to snub her, and she'd felt a little awkward at the lessons. And when she overheard one of the stable boys say she'd make a better pole dancer, she'd told her father she was tired of riding and wasn't up for any more lessons.

Desiree had later told her to stand tall, to not let anyone steal her joy. But they'd already stolen it. Riding just wasn't as much fun as it should have been.

Here on the ranch, though, with the horses out in the pasture, her interest had piqued again. And she realized another opportunity to ride had been provided her.

"Will you take me out someday?" she asked.

"Take you out?"

Did he think she meant on a date? Her cheeks warmed, and she tried to cool them off with a smile. "Yes. Horseback riding."

"I didn't know city girls were into horses."

"Some of us are."

"That surprises me."

She put her hands on her hips, rubbed her palms against the denim she wore. "Why?"

"It just does. That's all."

She wasn't sure what he was getting at, but it caused her pride to prickle. She'd been a tomboy for most of her early years. Then, when the kids at school started teasing her, Desiree and the other girls at Eddie's had given her a pep talk, followed by lessons on the application of makeup and the use of push-up bras and short skirts. "Take the power position," Desiree had said. "You've got the looks and the sexual appeal they're jealous of, so claim it proudly."

Chloe wouldn't share that with Jake, though. Instead, she asked, "How long has it been since you saddled a horse and rode all afternoon by yourself?"

"Too long, I suppose. I forgot how much I enjoyed it."

If he liked riding, one would think he'd naturally gravitate toward the ranch, yet that wasn't the case. Had he turned his back on the place somewhere along the way? Had his father and Desiree hoped he'd come to grips with whatever reasons he may have had for doing so?

Apparently, there was more to the man than met the eye. And what met her eye right now—raw, unbridled male—was intriguing in a primal way.

"I'm going to shower," he said. "When I'm done, I'm going to have a beer. I'll bring one for you, if you want to join me out here and maybe we can talk more…about horses."

"I'm not a beer drinker," she said.

He arched a dark brow, as though he didn't believe her.

But she didn't want him to renege on the invitation, so she added, "I might be able to handle a glass of wine, though."

"Fair enough."

As he turned to go, she stopped him. "So what do you say? Will you take me out riding someday? Or do I need to ask one of the hired hands?"

His brow furrowed, as though he was really struggling, but she didn't have it in her to go easy on him.

"All right. I'll take you out. Maybe tomorrow afternoon—if we get back from Dallas in time."

Brianna had an appointment in the morning with the psychologist.

"All right," she said. "But can we go early? I want to take her shopping, too. Every girl needs a new birthday dress."

"Then we'll have to leave first thing. Can you wake up that early?"

When she had to. Chloe grinned. "Don't worry about me. I'll be awake."

Ten minutes later the sun had set, yet Chloe remained on the darkened porch. The only light came from inside the living room, but she was content to stay outdoors with just the ranch sounds to keep her company.

"Help me out here, will you?"

Chloe turned to see Jake standing at the screen door, his hands holding a can of beer and a wineglass.

"Did you eat already?" she asked, as she helped him out.

"Not yet. I saw a plate on the stove. It'll keep." He handed her the glass of wine.

As their fingers brushed, her pulse skipped a beat. "Thanks."

"You're welcome." He flipped open the top of the can, yet didn't take a drink.

There were seats available on the porch, but he continued to stand, to survey the outbuildings and the corrals.

In the waning light, she still could see that he wore a white shirt, that his hair was damp from the shower.

He smelled of soap and a mountain stream, and she couldn't help being drawn to him. But it was more than his appearance tugging on her senses.

"Is something bothering you?" she asked.

"I, uh…" He cleared his throat. "Yeah, I guess you could say that."

"Can I help?"

"I don't know." He turned, studied her a moment. "I should have given Desiree a chance, but I didn't."

And now it was too late.

He didn't need to finish his sentence. Remorse lay heavy in his eyes.

"If it makes you feel better, Desiree wasn't one to hold a grudge."

He shrugged. "I'm not saying we could have been best friends, but I could have been nicer to her—not that I was ever rude. Still, I should have been more open-minded, more accepting. My dad had asked me to, but I…"

She could have primed him to continue, but waited, let him choose his words.

"As a kid, I missed not having a mom. And when I was finally introduced to mine, I wanted her to like me. I tried my damnedest to make her proud."

"Was she?" Chloe asked. "Proud of you?"

"Yeah, I think so." He lifted the can, looked at it, but still didn't take a swig. "Desiree was so different, so…I don't know. Maybe it bothered me that my dad was so damn happy with her but he hadn't been with my mom."

"You know," Chloe said, "Desiree was far more understanding than most people I know. And she made it clear to me that you would come around, so I don't think she would have held anything against you."

"Maybe you're right." He didn't seem convinced.

Chloe turned, placed a hand on his cheek, felt the light bristles he hadn't shaved this morning. "Believe me, Jake. She had high hopes for you. I understand you feeling a loss, but don't let the guilt drag you down. If she were here right now, she'd tell you herself."

Jake placed his hand over hers, holding her touch against his jaw. "Thanks."

"For what?"

"For not chewing me out. For understanding."

Their gazes locked, and a flood of emotion swept over her—desire, compassion, feelings she couldn't even put her finger on. He felt it, too, she suspected. A shared intimacy they'd never experienced before. A connection of some kind.

He lowered his head, as though he meant to brush an appreciative kiss across her lips, and her heart began to pound out a primal beat.

Fight or flight? her adrenaline demanded.

Cutting bait was her usual option when her feelings lay this raw, when her hormones threatened to take her down the wrong path with the wrong man.

And Jake was *so* not her type. *So* not…

So…

She ought to pull away, ought to break the spell.

Instead her lips parted and she lifted her mouth to his.

Chapter Eight

The kiss began slowly, sweetly—until a zesty taste of peppermint and a whiff of soap and musk sent Chloe's senses spinning.

She whimpered, yet didn't pull away. She couldn't. Instead, she placed her glass of wine on the porch rail, hoping she'd set it squarely on the flat surface, and turned toward Jake. He must have placed his can of beer somewhere, because he wrapped both arms around her and drew her close.

Their tongues touched, sleek and hot, then dipped and swirled. Something magical rushed through her, a wave of possibilities so real, so deep, so strong, that another woman, one who allowed herself to dream of romance, might have drowned in it.

As it was, Chloe could scarcely catch her breath.

She'd never kissed a man like this before, never had the urge to hold on tight and savor the moment until it swept her away.

As Jake caressed her back, her hips, she couldn't help but lean into him and press her body against his growing erection.

He wanted her.

And she wanted him, too.

The strength of her own arousal surprised her, and if he hadn't been holding her so close, she feared her knees would wobble from the sensual assault of his mouth, his hands. She needed to catch her breath, to gain control of her runaway desire. But she wasn't having any luck.

There were a hundred reasons why she ought to end things before they got out of hand, why a romantic relationship with Jake wouldn't work. Yet she'd seen the emotion in his expression, the remorse in his eyes earlier. And she knew his feelings ran deep.

She wasn't sure how far she'd let the kiss go, but she was tempted to let it go on forever. As he shifted, she followed suit. Her elbow brushed against something—no telling what. She didn't give it another thought until the sound of shattering glass caused them both to jump.

"Oops," she said. "My wineglass fell."

"Damn," he muttered.

She couldn't tell if he was complaining about broken glass, the interruption of the kiss or something else.

When it seemed as though he wasn't going to explain, she blew out the breath she'd been holding.

The kiss had been so sweet, so moving, so… unlike anything she'd ever experienced before, that her ability to think or reason seemed to have disappeared—for good. And she realized the loss of conscious thought wasn't a bad thing. Her feelings were too strong, too charged, too close to the surface.

Their bodies no longer touched, but his gaze held her transfixed. Shouldn't one of them say something? Confess something?

Gosh, she'd feel better if he would just make a joke and laugh it off.

Well, not really. She didn't know what she expected him to say or do, but she wasn't going to touch the subject of that kiss with a ten-foot pole until he did. She'd had her hopes dashed too many times in the past and wouldn't set herself up for embarrassment or heartbreak. So, as far as she was concerned, the ball was in his court.

Jake raked a hand through his hair. Damn. What in the hell had he done? And he wasn't talking about the broken glass.

Early this morning, the chat he'd had with Chloe about Desiree had left him unsettled, uneasy. So he'd spent the rest of the day on horseback, roaming the hills in search of peace—and not finding much.

The ride was supposed to have cleared his head, but when he returned to the ranch and found Chloe standing on the porch, just as natural and as pretty as you please, it almost felt as though he'd come home.

How weird was that?

In the kitchen, dinner was waiting for him. And here on the porch he had a beer he hadn't even touched. There was reason enough to withdraw into his own shell, yet all he could think about was spilling his guts out to Chloe, telling her about his mother and how hard he'd tried to please her.

The trouble was, in spite of his efforts, he still wasn't that close to his mom. So why even open that can of worms? Hell, he ought to be the one talking to the psychologist tomorrow—not Brianna.

Earlier this morning, and then again this evening when he'd stumbled onto the subject again, he'd tried to reel it in, but Chloe seemed to have understood what little he'd shared, as well as all he'd kept to himself.

When she'd reached over and cupped his cheek, when she'd looked at him with those pretty green eyes, he'd tripped up, thrown caution to the wind and to his raging hormones.

He'd kissed her. And what a kiss. A guy could go wild waiting for an instant replay to that.

"I'm sorry about breaking the glass," Chloe said.

To hell with the wineglass. How did a man go about backpedaling? All Jake needed was to have Chloe think there was more to that kiss than lust. And there wasn't. He was just caught up in the rush. That's all.

"I should have taken time to put it someplace

else," she added. "It's just that, well, I wanted my hands free." Her smile revealed a pair of dimples that made her appear innocent and virginal.

"Don't worry about it," he said, combing his hand through his hair—again. Damn. He hoped she wasn't into reading body language. "I'm the one who should apologize."

"For what?"

"For getting sentimental on you. And for kissing you."

"You don't need to apologize for that."

For which? he wondered. His feelings? Or the kiss? He didn't want Chloe to think he was going soft on her—emotionally speaking, of course. His response to her kiss had been anything but.

"You know," he said, picking up his can of beer. "I think I'd better get in the kitchen and eat that dinner before Mrs. Davies thinks I don't want it and throws it out."

"And I'd better pick up the broken glass before someone gets hurt."

"Good idea."

Jake didn't want to see anyone get hurt—not just by shards of glass, but by some lust-based pseudorelationship that didn't stand a snowflake's chance in hell. And if he and Chloe even considered taking things to a sexual level, the one with the greatest risk of getting hurt—or of being disappointed—was Brianna.

"What time do you want to leave for Dallas in the morning?" she asked.

"No later than nine." As he turned to open the screen door, hoping to leave the memory of the heated, blood-pounding kiss they'd just shared on the porch, it dogged him into the house.

He couldn't let something like that happen again. Usually, ending a relationship with a woman wasn't a problem for him. He was honest from the get-go, letting his dates know he didn't make commitments. But kissing Chloe hadn't been part of his plan.

And neither had his physical response as their tongues mated, as her body melded to his.

Under usual circumstances, he was good at distancing himself from a woman.

But how was he supposed to do that when they had to live in the same house for the next five weeks?

At four-thirty in the morning, Chloe rolled out of bed and called it a night. Sometimes sleeping was tough enough, but after fate had thrown a heart-stopping, world-spinning kiss into the mix, she hadn't stood a chance.

No matter how hard she tried, she couldn't stop thinking, stop reliving each heated touch, each breath-stealing moment.

She made her bed, then padded into the bathroom, intent on showering. When she glanced into the mirror, saw the rat's nest that had once been her hair and the dark circles under her eyes, she groaned.

"Darn you, Jake Braddock."

The least he could have done was said something more than, "I'm sorry."

She was sorry, too. Sorry that the best kiss she'd ever been a part of hadn't meant anything to him.

But what if he'd told her that the kiss had knocked his socks off, as well? What if he'd said that he wanted to... Well, that he wanted to see where the kiss might lead them?

If truth be told, Chloe hadn't had much luck in the male-female-relationship department. So what were the chances that something would pan out between a free spirit like her and a stuffed shirt like Jake?

Slim to none.

If they lived in the same state, the odds might be slightly better, but they were both established thousands of miles away from each other.

Long-distance relationships were tough, and there was no way Chloe would leave Bayside. Not with her business and properties there. And not when she was just beginning to gain the respect she'd been striving for all of her life.

As soon as she fulfilled her obligation at the ranch, she would take Brianna back to California with her.

Jake might not like it, but Desiree had made it clear that she wanted Chloe to be her daughter's guardian. The six-week stay at the ranch must have been a ploy to make Jake see reason and not present any problems or to contest the will. And if he decided not to give up custody of Brianna to Chloe freely, then the third party must have orders from Desiree to make sure everything worked out according to plan. So when all was said and done, they'd part ways.

So why pin her hopes on an unexpected kiss, especially one he'd felt the need to apologize for?

After a shower and a shampoo, she put on her makeup, using some cover-up under her eyes. It wasn't much help.

Deciding a bit of caffeine would do her some good, she wrapped the bath towel around her head and slipped on the clothes she'd slept in: a pair of black boxer shorts and a gray tank shirt. She would make a quick pot of coffee before anyone else woke up, then carry a cup back to the bathroom while she finished doing her hair, putting on a bit more makeup and getting dressed for the day.

But when she entered the kitchen, she realized she wasn't the only one up early.

Jake stood at the sink, the coffee carafe in his hand and the water running.

When she entered the room, he glanced over his shoulder, his eyes scanning her up and down. "Is that what you're wearing today?"

"Of course not. This is what I wore last night."

"Is that your idea of sleepwear?"

She looked down at the tank shirt. "What's wrong with it?"

"Nothing." He returned to his task of filling the carafe with water.

She leaned against the doorjamb. "I'll bet I'm wearing more than what you sleep in."

"That's different." He shut off the spigot, then faced her. "I would never come out into the kitchen in the raw."

Too bad, she thought. He probably looked pretty good with his clothes off. But she didn't want him to think she'd given it a second thought. "Don't worry. As soon as a cup of coffee has filtered through the grounds, I'll head back to my room and leave you alone."

"You're here now. You may as well wait until it's finished brewing." He carried the carafe to the coffeemaker and filled the well. Then he opened the canister and began to scoop out the grounds.

"Tell me something," she said to his back.

Jake paused in front of the can, holding a full scoop, waiting for her to finish her sentence. When she didn't, he turned. "What?"

She stood there, with a towel turban on her head, nipples beading through the thin fabric of her tank shirt, her long legs barely covered by boxer shorts. "Is there something about my body you find disagreeable?"

Wrong? With her body?

Hell, no. "I imagine you've been told a million times how beautiful you are, how shapely."

"Actually, I get a lot of wolf whistles and that sort of thing. But no one has actually said it and meant it."

"Then maybe you ought to take yourself more seriously."

"What do you mean?"

"Don't try so hard. Leave a little to a man's imagination."

She blinked, and he could have sworn he saw her suck in a breath. "I had no idea you were out here. If I had, I would have dressed. But you're acting as though I came out wrapped in a towel."

"If you had, you would have been more covered up."

She folded her arms. "All right. Enough is enough. It's not my clothes that have you all knotted up inside, it's your reaction to them."

"Is that what you think?" He chuffed, yet the truth she'd uncovered grated on him.

"Yes, it is. So maybe it's time we talked about that kiss we had last night."

He bristled. "What about it?"

"On a scale of one to ten—" she threw down the words like a gauntlet "—do you know what I'd score it?"

It had been an eleven, as far as he was concerned, but he'd rather die than admit it. Still, he wanted to know how high she'd rated it. And he wondered how many kisses she had to sort through to give it a rank.

He didn't say anything, though. He just waited for her to continue.

She cinched her arms tighter and shifted her weight to one bare foot. "I gave it a nine—at first."

A nine, huh? That wasn't too bad. A grin tugged at his lips. "What do you mean by 'at first'?"

"It slipped to a seven when you went indoors last night. And now it's a two."

"Why's that?"

"You've been a jerk ever since you kissed me. And now you want to pretend that it never happened."

"It would have been better if it hadn't."

"You're undoubtedly right." She pushed away from the door frame and straightened. "But the least you can do is to admit that it *did* happen. And that even though we'd be more likely to spot Elvis in Dallas this afternoon than to see anything come of it, at least as far as kisses went, it wasn't too bad."

Then she turned on her heel and strode away, leaving Jake and the coffee she'd come for in the kitchen.

He tried to ignore her words, as well as her abrupt departure, but she'd been right. He'd been an ass.

When the fresh brew filled the carafe, he filled a mug. He'd watched her yesterday morning, saw her pour in a splash of cream and add a spoonful of sugar, so he followed suit. Then he carried it to her room and knocked lightly on the door.

She answered, wearing a robe. *Only* a robe, he suspected, since he could see no sign of the tank shirt she'd had on before. Her hair was still wrapped in a towel.

"You forgot your coffee." He handed the mug to her.

Her lips parted, but she took it from him, holding the cup with both hands. "Thanks."

"I'm sorry for being a jerk," he said.

"Apology accepted."

He nodded, then started to walk away—until he had a second thought and decided to come clean on that, as well. "Oh. And for the record?"

She stared at him over the rim of the mug.

"I thought the kiss was off the charts."

Then he strode back to the kitchen, leaving them both to deal with the truth.

Chloe had remained in her room until it was almost time to leave, and Jake wondered if she was going to come out, at all.

He suspected she hadn't slept much last night. He'd noticed that she'd tried to mask the puffiness under her eyes with makeup.

Had memories of that kiss kept her awake as it had him?

Or had she been struggling with the insomnia that sometimes plagued her?

After a quick breakfast of toasted-oat cereal and banana muffins, they all piled into Jake's Navigator and drove into the city. They were both cordial, yet it seemed as though neither the kiss nor the apology had happened, which should have pleased him.

Yet for some reason, it didn't.

Along the way, Brianna's playful chatter kept them entertained and the conversation light. Still, the feel of Chloe in his arms, the heat of her whimper in his mouth, was never far from Jake's thoughts.

Whenever he slid a glance her way, when he sensed her eyes on him, he was sorely tempted to kiss her again and see if it was even better than he remembered.

Instead, he kept his eyes on the road, his hands on the wheel.

Once in the city, he drove to Galleria Dallas and stopped in front of the entrance to Nordstrom. "Is forty-five minutes going to give you two enough time?"

"Yes," Chloe said, "but aren't you going to help us pick out a pretty dress for Brianna's party?"

Jake wasn't big on shopping, especially with women. Yet he ought to agree, just to make sure Chloe chose something appropriate for the country-club set. But he had something he needed to do—alone. "No, that's okay. You two go ahead. I've got an errand to run. I'll meet you back here at a quarter to eleven."

"All right." Chloe reached for the child's hand. "Come on, Breezy."

Jake waited until they were out of sight, then drove through town until he reached the campus of Raleigh Academy, where he had an appointment to meet with the principal at ten o'clock.

The rolling green lawns and redbrick buildings looked much the same as they did when Jake had attended, although the place seemed barren without any children striding through the halls on their way to the playground.

He glanced at his watch, glad to know he'd made it with time to spare. He didn't want to be late, since there was a waiting list of applicants wanting to get in. Fortunately, he'd been able to pull a few strings and had gotten the principal to at least consider Brianna's application.

Once inside the school office, he removed his Stetson and introduced himself to the secretary, a tall, slender woman with bleached blond hair.

"I'll let Mrs. Walters know you're here," the woman said.

Jake took a seat in the reception area, but he didn't have to wait long. Mrs. Walters, a matronly brunette dressed in a navy blue business suit, greeted him with a smile and a slow Southern drawl. "Mr. Braddock?"

"Yes, ma'am." He stood and extended his hand. "How do you do?"

"Quite well, thank you." Mrs. Walters had an assertive grip, which shouldn't surprise him. He'd been told she ran a tight ship. "Won't you please come with me?"

Jake followed her down the hall and into a big, roomy office with a window that overlooked the courtyard, where children would eat their lunch once school began in the fall. Her mahogany desk, polished to a glossy shine, was meticulous, with everything appearing to have a place.

She took a seat in a beige leather chair, her back to a floor-to-ceiling bookcase that displayed several trophies and a couple of figurines, along with an impressive number of books.

Mrs. Walters clasped her pudgy, well-manicured hands on the desk in front of her. "So, I understand you'd like to enroll your niece in our school."

"Actually," Jake said, correcting her, "Brianna is my five-year-old sister. I'm her guardian."

Okay, so she wasn't quite five and Jake didn't have official custody yet, but it was really just a matter of time. It wouldn't take a psychologist to know Jake would be the better parent, although that's exactly who he still suspected the "third party" was.

"Please tell me why you chose our school," Mrs. Walters said.

Jake leaned back in his seat. "Raleigh Academy's reputation, for one thing. I also attended sixth, seventh and eighth grade here, so I have firsthand knowledge of the academic and social standards. But more importantly, I'd like my sister to have every advantage that this school can provide."

There was more to it than that, though.

Jake also wanted Brianna to attend the prestigious academy because of the social connections she'd make. Her friends and playmates would be the children of the upper echelon of Dallas society. In addition, he hoped to convince the psychologist that it was in Brianna's best interest to remain in Texas—with him.

"There is a rather involved application process," Mrs. Walters said. "We have the usual paperwork, of course, which I'll give you to complete and return. She'll also have to take a readiness test. As you know, the school has high academic standards."

Jake nodded. He wanted the best for his sister. And he wanted her to reach her full potential.

"We also require an interview with the child, as

well as a home visitation to meet the entire family," Mrs. Walters added.

A home visitation?

While Jake was glad that Raleigh Academy didn't accept just anyone, even if they could afford the stiff tuition, he wasn't keen on having someone from the school come out to the ranch and meet Brianna's "family." At least not during the next five weeks.

He forced a smile. "Of course. I can understand that."

What would Mrs. Walters think of the sexy red-head who was now living with them? Not much, he suspected, and Brianna would get blackballed before the conservative principal could clamp her gaping jaw shut.

"Maybe we can schedule the home visitation in August," Jake said. "Brianna and I will be staying out at our ranch near Granger for most of the summer, but we'll be back in the Dallas area by then."

"We don't mind going out of our way for a visitation. Besides, all of our decisions must be made before the board meeting at the end of July."

"I see." Jake would have to worry about the visitation later. Right now he was glad to pick up the paperwork and to set up the appointment for Brianna's testing and her interview.

"Once I receive your completed application packet," Mrs. Walters said, "I'll call and schedule the visit."

"All right." Jake slid her a no-problem grin, although something told him he was going to really have to work on Chloe. He couldn't risk having her screw things up. From what he'd already seen, she could sure turn the tables on him when she wanted to. And he couldn't afford to let that happen.

He'd just have to try and buy off Chloe that day with a shopping spree in Dallas. And speaking of shopping, he'd better get back to the mall to pick them up. There was no telling what she'd purchased or what had been going on while he'd left them alone.

Chapter Nine

As the young, stylishly dressed salesclerk totaled the charges, Chloe glanced at her silver bangle watch. She was running late, and Jake was probably waiting outside. It wasn't her intent to set him off before they went to see the psychologist, but with each second that passed the likelihood increased.

In the long run, she hoped he would be happy with her purchases.

She wasn't sure what he'd say about her needing to fly to Bayside tomorrow. Or her plan to take Brianna with her. Ten minutes ago, she'd received a call from her attorney, saying her meeting with the Bayside Redevelopment Committee had to be rescheduled, and since there was another pressing matter for them to discuss, they opted to move it up a week. If Chloe could get the committee members to see the wisdom in what she wanted to do with the Belmont Arms, her meeting with the planning department ought to be smooth sailing.

"Will this be all?" the salesclerk asked.

"Yes, it is."

"Then that'll be $168.43." Chloe handed the woman a VISA card, then turned to her pint-sized cohort. "What do you think, Breezy? The dress is pretty plain. I usually like bright colors."

"I think you should buy purple shoes to go with it." The minute the words were out, the little girl gasped. "Oh, no. I have a better idea. How about glass slippers?"

Chloe stroked the back of the Brianna's head, felt the silky strands of her hair. "Wouldn't Jake be surprised if I did?"

Brianna nodded. "And then we could buy some of them for me, too."

As planned, they had hit the children's department first, where they purchased a sundress for Brianna, a couple of shorts sets for play and a pair of pajamas. When Brianna had asked where they could find the fairy godmother and princess gowns, the good-natured clerk told them that the store hadn't ordered any this season, which she personally thought was a big mistake. "They're all the rage with girls your age," the woman said with a wink.

With twenty minutes to spare, Chloe had taken Brianna over to the women's section to kill some time. As she'd scanned the racks, she'd asked one of the sales associates on the floor to help her find something a Sunday-school teacher might wear.

Chloe told herself a classic white dress would be a nice addition to anyone's wardrobe, but if truth be told, she wanted Jake to know she could dress conservatively. That is, *if* she wanted to.

He'd suggested that when it came to her outfits, she should leave something to a man's imagination. So if a chic, white, knee-length dress played into his fantasy, so be it.

After signing the credit-card receipt, Chloe led Brianna out of the store and exited the mall.

"There he is," Brianna said, pointing to where Jake's SUV idled along the curb in a loading and unloading spot.

He sat in the driver's seat, his hat lowered to block the sun. Something told her he'd be grumpy about being kept waiting, but she supposed he'd get over it.

Once Chloe reached his vehicle, she knocked lightly on the window. He lifted his left arm and tapped on his wristwatch, letting her know she was late. Then he opened the door and got out of the car. The sound of Tim McGraw's latest hit played on the radio.

But other than his initial, mimed response, he kept his complaints to himself.

"Did you get your errands run?" she asked.

"Yep. How about you?" Jake scanned the bags she carried. "What'd you do, buy out the little girls' section?"

"We got new dresses, play clothes and pajamas," Brianna said.

Apparently, he assumed everything they'd purchased had been for Brianna, and Chloe decided not to suggest otherwise. Why stir him up if she didn't have to? She wasn't sure who Desiree had lined up to be the third party, the person to referee if she and Jake couldn't agree between them who should take custody of Brianna. But after much thinking about it, she suspected it might be the psychologist.

So why enter the doctor's office with either one of them in a foul mood?

While Chloe helped secure Brianna in the backseat of his Navigator, Jake placed their shopping bags in the rear.

"Are we going to see Dr. Rodgers now?" Brianna asked.

"We sure are." Jake slid behind the wheel, and when Chloe climbed into the passenger seat, he started the engine.

Ten minutes later they drove into the underground parking garage of a ten-story, gray-glass building.

"Can I punch the number eight when we get in the elevator?" Brianna asked.

"Sure, honey." Chloe glanced into the backseat. "Elevators are fun, aren't they?"

Once inside the doctor's office, they signed in with a receptionist, then sat in the waiting room, a comfortable sitting area decorated in shades of beige and blue.

"Want to see the fish?" Brianna pointed to a huge

tank built into the south wall. "Me and Mommy tried to count them once, but there are a whole bunch and they swim really fast."

Before they could scan the colorful tropical fish or comment on the ugly algae-eater, Dr. Rodgers came out and called Brianna's name.

He was a small, slight man, with thinning hair and bright-blue eyes. He introduced himself to Jake and Chloe, clearly aware of the child's current living arrangement.

"I'd like to see Brianna first," he said, "then I'll call the two of you back when we're finished."

As he began to lead the child back to his office, he said, "You ought to see my new toy chest, Brianna."

When the door shut, leaving Jake and Chloe in the waiting room, he whispered, "We're paying him to play *games* with her?"

"That's because she'll be more inclined to talk and share her feelings."

"How do you know that?"

She smiled. "Desiree told me. But I also took a child psychology class in college."

Jake cast a glance at her as though he seemed surprised she had an education. She hadn't gotten a degree, though. But she wouldn't offer that information. "There's a lot about me that you don't know."

"I'm sure there is." He took a seat on the blue-plaid sofa, then sorted through several magazine on the coffee table, choosing a *Field and Stream* over several issues of *Highlights* and other publication for children. As he began to thumb through the pages, he paused to study an ad for fishing reels.

Chloe couldn't help commenting, "I thought you were a city boy and didn't like the outdoors."

"I wouldn't say that, but I do like to fish. It's been ages since I took the time, though."

"When did you last go fishing?"

"About a year before my dad died—on Father's Day. He and I rode out to the old Riley place. It's owned by a friend of his, but no one lives there anymore. About a mile to the east of the house, there's a private lake that's chock-full of trout." He smiled wistfully. "We caught a ton and ate until we were stuffed that night. It was the best I've ever tasted."

"It sounds like a special day."

His gaze locked on hers. "It was. My dad and I spent the afternoon together, cleaned and filleted our catch, then grilled them and ate our fill."

"Where was Desiree?"

He paused, reflecting. "She cooked it all up."

"The fish?"

"No. The father/son day. She said that she and Brianna had celebrated with my dad the night before." He grew even more pensive.

Had he just realized how badly Desiree had wanted her family to be whole and happy?

"After dinner," Jake said, "we sat out on the back porch and talked about all kinds of things."

"Like what?"

"Whether the Texas Rangers stood a chance in the

playoffs or whether a guy ought to use a nine iron off the sixth tee at the country club." He grew quiet again, then seemed to shrug it off. "Like I said, it was a good day."

Chloe let him ponder the memory and reached for a magazine of her own.

It didn't seem very long before Dr. Rodgers returned. "Brianna is going to help Miss Mary, my secretary, color some pictures while we chat."

Jake and Chloe stood and followed the doctor back to his office.

"How's she doing?" Chloe asked.

"She seems to be dealing with her loss fairly well. At her age, death is still a difficult concept."

"There have been a few sad times," Jake said, "especially late in the evenings. Chloe has sat up with her, which seems to help."

The way he'd said it, like one loving parent talking about another, touched her. Were they becoming teammates with the same goal?

"It sounds as though your living situation is working out okay," the doctor said.

"So far so good." Jake sat back in his chair and stretched out his legs, as though comfortable with it all. "I do plan to hire a nanny."

"Why?" Chloe asked. "We're doing fine without one. Besides, Mrs. Davies has been a great help."

"I'm talking about later," he said, "when our stay at the ranch is done. I've checked with an agency that provides nannies with impeccable references."

Was he assuming that Chloe would return to California and leave Brianna with him? If so, he was wrong.

But rather than argue in front of the psychologist, Chloe merely said, "I don't like the idea of Brianna being raised by hired help."

"I'm not talking about a babysitter," Jake said. "The nanny would have a degree in child development. She'd be a professional. And she'd only be involved with Brianna while I was at the office."

Chloe wanted to leap up and tell him that a nanny was out of the question. Instead she gripped the armrest of her chair, her nails biting into the fake-leather fabric.

"I've also talked to Bernadette Walters, the principal at Raleigh Academy," Jake added. "There's a good chance Brianna will be able to attend school there in the fall."

Chloe's stomach clenched. He wanted to put her in a private school? No way.

Memories of her own experience at Preston Prep swept over her, and she opened her mouth to object, to cry out about the way she'd been treated. But here? In front of a psychologist who might decide she was still struggling with those issues and might not make a good guardian for Brianna?

She took a deep breath, then slowly let it out. "There are some very good schools in Bayside, as well as San Diego."

"Speaking of Bayside," the doctor said, "Brianna is excited about flying back there with you tomorrow.

She told me all about her new friends, Jenny and Penny."

Chloe risked a glance at Jake, who looked as though he was about to shoot up out of his chair.

"What are you talking about?" he asked. "Did you say tomorrow?"

"I have a business meeting I need to attend. We'll only be gone for a couple of days."

"Why didn't you say anything?"

"I just received word a little while ago. I haven't had a chance to mention it."

She probably could have sent Ron, her attorney, in her place, even though he thought it was better if she met with the Redevelopment Committee in person. But right now she also needed to get back on her own turf so she could regroup and come up with a game plan. One that didn't include throttling Jake with her bare hands the moment the good doctor left the room.

How dare he think she'd step aside and let him raise Brianna—especially when he started talking about nannies and prestigious private schools.

"We're supposed to stay on the ranch," Jake said. "Remember?"

She hadn't forgotten, but it seemed as though he was making plans without consulting her. "Under the circumstances, I'm sure Desiree would have been flexible." Especially if she'd understood why Chloe needed to go back home. "Besides, Jake. It will only be for two days. Three at the most."

"Then, at least leave Brianna home with me."

The doctor cleared his throat. "If the two of you are going to come to some kind of agreement on joint custody and parenting, you'll need to find a way to work through these little setbacks."

Little setbacks? Is that what you called irreconcilable differences?

Silence stretched between them like a brand-new rubber band.

"When are you leaving?" Jake asked.

"Tomorrow at noon." She hadn't purchased any tickets yet, but she would. Just as soon as she got some time alone.

"And when will you be back?"

"We'll only need to spend two nights there."

Jake slunk in his seat, clearly not happy. Yet she wondered if he was trying to keep his cool in front of the doctor.

When the hour-long appointment was up and they left the office, they headed to his car.

"I'm hungry," Brianna said.

"Okay." Jake opened the rear passenger door for his sister. "Let's stop someplace and have lunch."

Quite frankly, Chloe's stomach was in knots, and she'd be lucky if she could keep down anything. But Brianna needed to eat.

Once they were on the road and headed to the nearest fast-food restaurant, Jake asked, "We'll make this quick. I assume you still want to saddle a couple of horses when we get back and go for a ride."

As much as she'd looked forward to horseback

riding, she didn't need to ponder the wisdom of that for very long.

"I think I'll pass."

No matter how handsome he was, Jake Braddock was her opponent—not her friend.

Jake refused to fight, and decided to give in to Chloe's trip and to her taking Brianna. Why should he put up a fight guaranteed to upset Brianna when he had the psychologist in the palm of his hand? So the next twenty-four hours had been uneventful and quiet, except for Brianna's enthusiasm about going back to California for a visit.

She told him she was looking forward to seeing her friends, Jenny and Penny, as well as Chloe's cat, which he'd learned was being boarded by a neighbor.

When Dr. Rodgers had mentioned Chloe's plan to take Brianna to Bayside, huge red flags had gone up immediately. He still didn't know what in the hell she was up to.

A business meeting, she'd said.

Of course, Jake had things to do, too—work at the office, reports and projects he'd been postponing or delegating to others. And Chloe's trip gave him a reason to leave the ranch, as well. So he ought to be glad she was going to be in California for a few days.

But he wasn't. He didn't trust her.

After seeing Brianna and Chloe off at the airport the next morning, Jake headed to his office. All the while, he felt uneasy and found it hard to focus on his tasks at hand.

What was she really doing in the San Diego area? What was so pressing?

When he'd asked, she'd simply repeated it was a business meeting. And even though he knew she had a dance studio, she really didn't seem to be the businesswoman type.

She'd also mentioned the schools in Bayside.

Now the red flags that had already risen in his mind were flapping madly and doubling in size.

Surely, she wouldn't go so far as to enroll Brianna without telling him about it.

Okay, so he was guilty of doing the same thing. But as far as private schools went, Raleigh Academy was the cream of the crop, and if she saw the campus or met the teachers, she would have to agree.

He managed to get a few things squared away at the office, but his mind wasn't on work. So he picked up a bite to eat at his favorite sports bar and grill, then spent the night at his town house. It was great to be back in his own bed again.

But he'd slept like crap.

At six in the morning Jake called American Airlines and secured a direct flight to San Diego. He also lined up a rental car to use. Then he drove to the airport.

He would feel a whole lot better when he found out what was going on in Bayside.

Once Jake had landed at Lindbergh Field and picked up a rental car, he drove to the Ocean Breeze Condominiums, a Spanish-style complex with white stucco walls, red tiled roofs and wrought-iron fencing. The rolling green lawns were dotted with palm trees and hibiscus loaded with yellow, red and pink flowers.

He'd only been here once, briefly, but he found Chloe's condo and parked in a space reserved for visitors. A woven welcome mat, flanked by two clay pots of red geraniums, sat at the front door.

He knocked, then rang the bell.

Footsteps—an adult, he suspected—sounded from within. He expected to see Chloe, but his smile bottomed out when a well-built, thirtysomething guy with wheat-colored hair opened the door. His navy blue shirt said Bayside Fire Department in white block letters.

"I…" Did Jake have the wrong house? He could have sworn number 146 was the right one. "I'm looking for Chloe Haskell."

"She's not here at the moment."

"Who are you?" Jake asked.

The guy stiffened. "Maybe you should tell me who *you* are first."

"I'm Jake Braddock, Brianna's brother."

The fireman grinned. "Joe Davenport. We talked on the phone when I called your place looking for Chloe." Then he stuck out a hand as though Jake had just proven that he wasn't a door-to-door salesman or a bill collector. "Come on in."

As Jake stepped into Chloe's condominium, his attention was immediately caught by the sight and sound of a baseball game on television, as well as the aroma of something chocolate baking in the oven. Since he hadn't eaten this morning, the chocolate won out. "What's she making?"

"Actually, Chloe and Brianna went to Horton Plaza, but they'll be back shortly. And as for the goodies, our oven is on the blink at home. We've got a new one ordered, but my wife had committed to making cupcakes for a Boy Scout function, so Chloe let me come over here and borrow her kitchen." Joe laughed. "Don't tell anyone, but they're already baked and frosted. I'm still hanging out because the game is all tied up and I want to see who wins."

At the cracking sound of a bat striking a ball and the subsequent roar of the crowd, both men turned to the television screen.

"It's outta here," the announcer yelled. "The Padres take the lead in the top of the ninth."

After an instant replay, the station cut to a commercial.

"Do you live around here?" Jake asked.

"I used to. When my wife and I learned we were expecting the twins, we sold the condo and moved to a bigger home a couple of blocks away."

"How long have you known Chloe?"

"Several years. She's a good friend. My wife, Kristin, and I have been house-sitting for her while she was gone."

His wife, huh? Something told Jake that Chloe didn't have many female friends. "Your wife doesn't have a problem with you being at Chloe's by yourself?"

"Why would she?"

Jake shrugged. "Some women might consider Chloe a threat."

Joe chuckled. "Actually, when Kristin first met Chloe, she wasn't too keen on us being friends. But when she got to know her, she realized Chloe is one of the most honest, kindhearted people you'll ever meet. Underneath that flashy surface, she's a loving woman who's dead set on saving the world, at least, in a bless-the-beasts-and-the-children sense."

"I'm beginning to see that," Jake said. "I've seen her scoop a spider out of the bathtub and carry it to safety."

"That's our Chloe. She also serves meals to the homeless at a shelter downtown, delivers food to shut-ins, fosters stray cats for an animal-rescue organization and travels to Mexico with a group that builds orphanages and homes for the needy."

"I guess that doesn't leave her much time for herself."

"She's pretty busy. I told her she ought to open up an office and hire a personal secretary, just to keep track of her projects."

"Doesn't she work at the dance studio?"

"Some. But she's hired a manager to run things for her. She goes in several days a week."

Jake wondered how she supported herself and all her charities but didn't ask. There was no need for

Joe to suspect him of digging for information about her, even though he was. "She mentioned having a meeting with the planning department."

"That's not for a couple of weeks," Joe said. "She's trying to purchase an old, run-down apartment building on East Third, and she has an idea that would help renovate several other properties nearby."

"But I was under the impression that she had something else going on. A meeting today."

"Oh, yeah. That's at three this afternoon. She has an opportunity to talk to the Bayside Redevelopment Committee. If she can convince them to back her ideas—which are a bit unusual but just might work—the meeting with the planning department ought to be a slam dunk."

Quite frankly, Jake was still trying to sort it all out. But it ought to be easy to convince her to let him have full custody of Brianna when the required six weeks were over. After all, she'd established herself in San Diego, where she had a business, friends and a pseudofamily of sorts.

Heck, she probably had a boyfriend. Maybe a slew of them.

"Is she seeing anyone?"

"Not that I know of." Joe eyed him as though he suspected Jake would like to be in the running. "Why?"

"Just wondered." He wasn't sure why he asked. But the fact that she wasn't dating anyone, at all, was surprising. "I figured a sexy woman like her has to beat men off with a stick."

"She attracts plenty of interest, but her dates rarely get to the let's-get-naked stage."

"You gotta be kidding." The woman exuded sexuality. Just looking at her would give some men an erection.

"Chloe might dress like she's been around the block, but she's pretty innocent in the relationship department."

That was hard—no, make that *impossible* to believe. No one could dress that suggestively and still be sexually naive.

Still, he found the idea intriguing. Just like when a math professor would place a problem on the board and say that only the top students would be able to solve it. Jake had always been one of the first to take a crack at it.

When a knock sounded, Joe answered. "Hey, Pete. How's it going?"

"Mary is in the middle of preparing scalloped potatoes for the luau tonight and asked me to come over and borrow some milk from Chloe. Ours is outdated."

"I'll check and see if Chloe has any she can spare. If so, I'm sure she won't mind."

When Joe went to the kitchen, the elderly man eyed Jake intently, so Jake introduced himself.

"Are you little Brianna's brother?" Pete asked.

Jake nodded.

"Cute kid. Too bad about her mother passing." Pete clucked his tongue and shook his head. "But at least she's got Chloe to look after her."

She had Jake, too, but he kept that to himself. He doubted Chloe's Bayside fan club would be happy to learn that he wasn't going to be giving up custody of his sister. He was, however, starting to feel much better about Chloe having occasional visitation.

Joe returned with the milk. "There's another half gallon, and since she'll be leaving again tomorrow, that ought to be enough."

"I'll talk to her tonight and offer to pay for what I took." Pete glanced at Jake. "It was nice meeting you. Are you going to join us this evening?"

"This is the first I've heard of the luau."

"Well, tell Chloe to bring you along. She's making her famous rainbow salad. If you haven't tried it, you're in for a treat." Pete shifted the jug of milk in his arms, leaving a wet spot on his green shirt. "Thanks, Joe."

When the neighbor left, Joe shut the door.

Another roar of the crowd caused them both to look at the television screen.

"That's it," the announcer said. "The Padres win, four to three. Join us after the commercial break, as we go live to the locker room."

"I guess I'd better get my cupcakes and go home," Joe said.

"All right." Jake took a seat on the sofa. "I'll watch

the after-game highlights while I wait for Chloe to return."

When Joe left, Jake reached for the remote, which was right next to a photo album on the coffee table. He meant to surf through the channels, but he couldn't help picking up the album and taking a peek. He was intrigued by the woman—now more than ever—and wanted to know more about her.

He flipped through the pictures she'd undoubtedly collected over the years.

There was one of her and Desiree at a buffet line. They were dressed like pilgrims and serving a hodge-podge of people. One old man in the snapshot had scraggly hair and no front teeth, but his smile was enough to light the room.

Jake wasn't sure when it had been taken, but Chloe appeared to be a teenager at the time.

There were several shots of a construction job. One showed Chloe on a ladder with a leather tool-belt cinched at her waist. The other was of her sitting under the shade of a tree, reading to several dark-haired children.

The more he looked, the more he saw a young woman who deserved his admiration. His respect.

Okay, so maybe he'd misjudged her. Misread her character. Maybe he ought to backpedal and use another approach with her. He was going to have to wipe the slate clean, though, which meant he'd have to turn on the charm. And if he was lucky, maybe she'd let him kiss her again.

He wouldn't mind scoring another nine in her mind, or trying for a perfect ten. And he just might find out how innocent she really was.

What would it hurt?

Chapter Ten

Timewise, Chloe was really pushing it to go shopping this morning, but when she'd unpacked the conservative white dress she'd purchased in Dallas, she'd had second thoughts about wearing it this afternoon.

Black might be a better choice for a business meeting, especially if she wanted to maintain the respect she was finally beginning to garner.

So she'd left Joe baking cupcakes at the house and taken Brianna to Horton Plaza. On a whim, she'd actually worn the white dress so she could tell the salesclerk she was looking for something similar in black.

"I can see why," the woman had said. "That dress

was made for a classy young woman. Come with me. I've got something that just came in, and I think it's exactly what you're looking for."

Now, as Chloe held Brianna's hand and carried a brand-new outfit by the plastic-draped hanger, they strolled through the mall on their way to the parking garage.

"Oh, look." Brianna pointed to a birthday party display in the front window of a toy store that could just as easily have been found in Toontown at Disneyland.

Chloe slowed her steps so the child could study the stuffed animals sitting around a small table-and-chair set. "How cute is that."

"I want balloons at my party, too," Brianna said.

"Of course. Let's have hundreds. We can put ribbon strings on the ends. If they're filled with helium, they'll gather on the ceiling during the party. And when your friends are ready to go home, they can take a bundle with them."

"Okay. And I want a great big birthday cake. Like a bride cake, with a big one on the bottom and little ones stacked way up on top."

"Absolutely. What flavor do you want? Chocolate?"

"I want *all* the flavors."

Chloe scrunched her nose. "I think that might taste yucky if we mix them all up."

"We don't have to mix them up. We can have strawberry on the bottom and chocolate on top of that and white on top of that. And then all the way up."

"Apparently, you've given your party a lot of thought," Chloe said.

"Uh-huh. And I told Jenny and Penny about it yesterday, when we went to their house, and I told them they could come."

"The party will be in Texas, so it's a long way for them to drive."

"Can't they fly in an airplane like we did?"

Donna Townsend, Jenny and Penny's mother, was a stay-at-home mom. As it was, the family was struggling to make it on one paycheck, so a trip for three to Texas would be a real hardship.

But Desiree's words came to mind. *It might be difficult for Brianna to celebrate this year.*

That was true, so Chloe would do whatever she could to make the day and the party special. If Donna was willing and able to bring the twins to Texas, Chloe would buy the tickets.

She gave the child's hand a gentle squeeze. "I'll talk to their mother about it."

Brianna gasped and pulled on Chloe's fingers. "Guess what? I got another good idea."

"What's that?"

"Since Jenny and Penny like Cinderella and Snow White, too, we could have a princess party. And Jake could make a castle for us to play in behind the barn."

The princess party sounded just fine, but something told Chloe that it was going to be tough to talk Jake into building a castle.

A grin tickled her lips. She couldn't wait to see the look on his face when Brianna put in her request, though.

"Never limit your options," Desiree used to say—*Lessons from Desiree* #14. So, as an alternative plan, as soon as they were back in Texas, Chloe planned to make some calls and see if she could rent one of those big, blow-up jumpy things. Surely somebody had one in the shape of a castle.

When they got back to the car, Chloe drove to Bayside. All the while she and Brianna discussed the princess-theme decorations.

"I know we already bought a dress for the party," Brianna said, "but maybe we can give it back to the store. I really want to wear a Cinderella gown. Do you think we could find a store that sells them?"

"I'm sure we can."

"And could I wear a crown, too?"

Chloe grinned. A faux tiara wouldn't be too tough to find. She'd seen cheapy ones at various drugstores. And she could probably buy a nicer one at a bridal shop in the flower girl section. "That shouldn't be a problem. I'll make a few calls when we get home."

Brianna let out an enthusiastic gasp. "I know. And we could try to get some glass slippers."

Now that would be pushing it. "I'm not sure where to find those, but I promise to look very hard."

As they turned into the Ocean Breeze complex, she had a thought. Pete, her neighbor, used to be a

Hollywood stuntman before he retired. Maybe he still had connections with someone in the costume department at one of the studios.

After parking the car, Chloe and Brianna headed to the condo. The front door was unlocked.

Chloe suspected Joe was still inside, since he was a stickler for safety. But she couldn't imagine why he would be. Those cupcakes should have been done an hour or more ago.

Uh-oh. She'd told Joe to make sure Miss Priss didn't get outdoors. Maybe he was looking for her. She hadn't been acting her usual self.

Mary and Pete, the next-door neighbors, had boarded the cat while Chloe was in Texas. They'd said she'd been shy and fussy, but ever since Chloe had brought her home yesterday, she'd been stand-offish. Chloe suspected the cat was angry about being left behind.

It had been tough deciding whether to take her to Texas or not. At her age, Miss Priss was pretty set in her ways.

Chloe turned the knob and swung open the door, only to find Jake seated on her couch.

When he shot her a sheepish grin, her breath caught and her pulse skipped a beat. "What are you doing here, Jake?"

"I—" His eyes widened and his lips parted. Appreciation glimmered in his eyes as he looked her over. "Wow. That's a nice dress."

She glanced down at what she'd worn shopping.

To be honest, she'd been in such a hurry to get out the door this morning she felt a bit windblown. Still, his compliment resonated in her ears, and she found it heartwarming. "Thank you."

"Are you wearing that to the meeting?" he asked.

"I thought I'd wear something else. Something black."

"You're not going in that skimpy little dress you wore to the attorney's office in Texas, are you?"

The sexy black knit?

"No." She'd never do that. This meeting was too important. "Why do you ask?"

"It's just that I figured you would want everyone to take you seriously, and that dress… Well, it's hard for a guy to keep his mind—" Jake glanced at Brianna and held back the rest of the sentence.

"Sometimes I like to be rebellious," Chloe admitted.

"I've come to that conclusion. But do you know what? You look great. I don't see any need for you to change your clothes."

She tended to be skeptical of Jake's comments and opinions, but she'd seen the respectful gaze in the salesclerk's eye today, as well as a couple of surreptitious looks from more than a few men she'd passed in the store. They'd all treated her like both a mother and a lady, and not once had someone raised an eyebrow or made a sexual innuendo.

"Why don't you dress like this more often?" Jake asked.

Because, when she was younger and tried to fit in

with the others at Preston Prep, it hadn't mattered what she'd done, what she'd worn. The hurtful comments and whispers had come at her when she least expected. But she'd found that when she wore short skirts and tight blouses, she was prepared for the petty jabs, which made her feel in control.

But Jake didn't need to know that. "I usually dress for comfort or to suit my mood."

"Well, you must be incredibly comfortable and in a good mood today. I like your hairstyle, too."

She touched the side of her head, felt the loose strands she'd pulled back, twisted and held with a clip. "I don't usually wear my hair this plain."

"Don't ever think of yourself as plain. The color alone is stunning and makes you stand out in a crowd."

Who *was* this guy? And what had he done with the real Jake?

He was being…sweet. Complimentary. And unless he was one heck of an actor, he seemed sincere. She wasn't sure how to deal with it.

"Thank you," she said again. Then she cleared her throat. "You didn't answer my question earlier. What are you doing here?"

"I finished every bit of pressing work at the office yesterday and figured that since we'd agreed to be a family for the time being, I should catch a flight and join you. So here I am."

That he was. All six-foot-plus of man and brawn. She placed her purse on the easy chair. "I'd better get ready or I'll be late for my meeting."

"I'll watch Brianna while you're gone. And then, maybe we can go out to dinner after you get back."

"But the luau is tonight," Brianna said. "And there's gonna be food there. And I already told Jenny and Penny I'm going."

Jake looked at Chloe. "What's the deal about the luau?"

"It's a community potluck with a Hawaiian theme. A couple of the neighbors are roasting a pig. It's become an annual event."

"Since it's a potluck," Jake said, "I'll run to the store and pick up some sodas and beer. That's my usual contribution to those kinds of things."

Apparently thinking the adults had decided against a restaurant, Brianna skipped to the bedroom in which she'd been staying.

As Chloe started toward her own room, she paused. "Have you seen my cat?"

"Are you talking about a crotchety gray tabby?" Jake asked.

Chloe nodded. "She's not big on strangers."

"Tell me about it." Jake pointed to the top of the hutch in the dining room, where Miss Priss crouched, watching them all with hawk eyes.

"Aw, Prissy. What am I going to do with you?" Chloe blew out a sigh. "Take you to Texas, I suppose. I should have never left you behind."

Jake grabbed the remote, turned off the television and got to his feet. "Are you forgetting about the dog you dragged home last week?"

"Not at all. It shouldn't be a problem."

"Are you crazy?" He stepped away from the couch and made his way toward her. "Haven't you ever heard the phrase, 'fighting like cats and dogs'? There's a reason it was coined."

He stood near her, close enough for her to catch a whiff of his woodsy scent. Close enough to make it hard for her to argue. After what seemed like forever, she said, "A scuffle or two when they first meet is to be expected, of course, but before you know it, Sweetie Pie and Miss Priss will learn to be friends."

"You make it sound easy."

Nothing seemed easy right now. Certainly not breathing or maintaining a regular heart rate. "It just takes time. And a little patience."

"How about for us?" Jake reached for her cheek, caught a strand of hair that had apparently fallen out of place and brushed it aside. His fingers, the knuckles, lingered on her cheek. "We started off on the wrong foot, Chloe. Do you think, with time and patience, we could become friends?"

"Of course." He used the word *friends* as though he meant it, yet his expression, his touch, suggested so much more.

The memory of the kiss they'd shared came to mind. On that particular night, they'd certainly seemed to be compatible, at least sexually. But it had been over before it began.

And something told her that anything romantic or

lasting between her and Jake would take more than just time and patience.

It was going to take a miracle.

The meeting with the redevelopment council had gone better than Chloe had expected. Once she'd explained what she wanted to do with the Belmont Arms as well as her plans to purchase the property next door, the group had been pleased.

"Turning that adult bookstore into a recreation room for the residents of the apartment building will be a definite improvement to the city," Harry Logan had said. "Do you think the owner of Triple-X-Stacy will sell?"

According to what Chloe had learned from Lucky Lewellyn, the Vietnam vet who knew just about everything going on in the seedy part of town, the owner of the building was in failing health and didn't trust anyone to manage the place for him.

"My attorney is preparing an offer," Chloe said, "and we expect the owner to give it some serious consideration."

The committee chair had nodded sagely. "We wish you the best of luck, Ms. Haskell."

Chloe returned home, just as the sun dropped toward the Pacific. As she neared her condo, many of the other residents of the complex had already begun to gather on the lawn.

Three men stood near a roped-off area, where a

pig roasted underground. The older gentleman was her neighbor, Pete, who spotted her car and waved.

Three long tables had already been draped with red plastic cloths and several women arranged the few bowls and platters that had arrived.

Several teenagers had strung a net across the grass near the laundry room and had set a volleyball in motion. It looked as though the first game would start soon.

As she left her vehicle in the carport and headed toward her condo, she spotted Brett Tanner fiddling with the cords of a boom box that would soon pipe in Hawaiian music to set the mood. She greeted the off-duty Navy helicopter pilot before making her way to the front door.

"How's Caitlin doing?" she asked.

"Much better now," Brett said. "I think she's finally over the morning sickness. She and Emily will be coming along as soon as her casserole is out of the oven."

"Good."

When Chloe reached her condo and stepped inside, Brianna ran to meet her. "I've been looking out the window, and it's time for the luau. When can we go outside?"

"Soon. I need to change my clothes, then I'll take our salad out of the fridge."

"How did the meeting go?" Jake asked, as he entered the living room.

"Very well." She kicked off her shoes, which was

usually the first thing she did whenever she got home. "The committee was very supportive and didn't foresee any problems from the city."

She unclipped her hair, then shook out the curls. When she finished, she glanced at Jake, saw him watching her. She gave a little shrug. "I've been dying to do that. My hair has been bound up all day."

So had her nerves. She'd been on edge all afternoon, determined to make a good impression. Of course, once she'd entered the room and begun to state her case, it all flowed naturally. Still it was nice to be home now and on her own turf.

Ten minutes later she'd changed into a pair of jeans and a black shirt and had reached into the linen closet and grabbed a blanket for them to sit on. Next she went to the kitchen, where she ran into Jake.

"Brianna and I went to the market while you were gone," he said. "I picked up soda and beer. They're cold, but should we keep them on ice?"

"There are usually several coolers near the dessert table," Chloe said, as she pulled her salad from the fridge. "If not, I've got one in the garage, and we can come back for it."

Minutes later they joined the neighbors who had begun to gather for the luau.

"Look," Brianna said, pointing to her friends who were standing near their mother. "Jenny and Penny are already here. Can I go and see them?"

Chloe waved at Donna. "Sure, Breezy. Go on ahead."

As Brianna skipped away, Chloe whispered to Jake, "She would really like Jenny and Penny to attend her birthday party. I'm not sure she realizes how far away Texas is or how difficult it will be for them to come."

"It's nice that she's made friends, though."

"I agree."

As Donna and the girls approached, Chloe introduced them to Jake.

The twins, whose only similarity was their rhyming names, studied Jake as though he were in costume, rather than dressed in black denim jeans and a blue button-down shirt.

Dark-haired Penny whispered to Brianna, "Is that your brother?"

Brianna nodded.

"How come he's so old?" the little blonde asked.

"'Cause he was born a long time ago," Brianna told them in a voice that was hushed but not silent.

As the girls began to chatter among themselves, Donna smiled at Jake. "I'm sorry about that. You know how kids are."

Jake returned her smile. "Don't worry about it. Our situation is a bit unusual. You can't expect kids to understand."

"Can Brianna spend the night at our house," Penny asked her mom. "Please?"

"It's all right with me, but you'll have to ask Chloe."

Brianna's excitement was hard to ignore. "Please, oh, please. I'll be good."

"Jake and I will talk it over, okay, Breezy? We're supposed to be learning how to coparent."

Donna chuckled. "In our house it's just the opposite. Sam has to work out of town so often that I end up making most of the decisions on my own. I'd much rather have him around."

As the sound of ukuleles began to play on the speakers set up along the perimeter and a refreshing ocean breeze blew through the palm leaves, causing the trees to sway, a tropical mood settled on the crowd.

"Why don't I take the girls to the playground while you unload the things you brought," Donna told Chloe.

"Okay. Thanks. I'll join you in a few minutes."

Chloe pointed Jake toward the coolers, where he deposited his beer and sodas. Then she placed her salad on the table.

"You can sit with us and watch the kids play for a while," she told him. "Unless you'd rather mingle."

He reached into the cooler and pulled out a soda. "I may wander over there in a few minutes, but I'll hang out here for now."

Chloe nodded, then headed for the playground.

Jake watched her go, watched the swish of her hips. Her sexy gait, which had always caught his attention before, seemed completely natural now. As much a part of her as her smile.

Earlier, when he'd seen her dressed in the classic black dress she wore to the meeting, her hair swept up into a professional twist, she'd looked like the kind of woman a guy wouldn't mind taking home to Mom. Even his own.

She'd been a bit nervous, but he couldn't understand why. She'd looked every bit like any competent businesswoman he'd ever known, and she clearly knew her stuff.

He'd cupped her jaw and caught her gaze. "You'll knock them dead with your intellect, as well as your appearance."

She'd slid him an appreciative grin, then covered his hand with hers, holding it to her cheek. "Thanks, Jake. You have no idea how much I appreciate that."

Then she'd headed to the door. As she left the house, he'd been further convinced that he wanted to get to know the real Chloe a whole lot better.

"Do they have any beer in that cooler?" a dark-haired, thirtysomething guy asked.

"Yep," Jake said. "At least a case of Buds and two six-packs of Corona."

"Good." The guy, who wore khaki slacks and a Tommy Bahama shirt, reached out his arm. "I'm Brett Tanner."

The men shook hands, and Jake introduced himself.

"Are you new to the neighborhood?" Brett asked. "I don't remember seeing you around."

"I'm just here for a couple of days. I'm Chloe's houseguest."

Brett popped the top of the can, then took a swig of beer. "I'm in the Navy and get deployed now and again, so it seems as though each time I come home there's someone new in the neighborhood."

They talked for a while about the choppers Brett flew, about how he loved his career, but missed his family when he was gone.

"That's my wife," Brett said, nodding toward a pretty blonde who'd just joined Chloe and Donna on a park bench overlooking the playground. "Her name is Caitlin. And that little girl in pigtails is our daughter, Emily."

As Jake and Brett continued to chat, they learned that they had a lot in common. A love of sports for one, fishing for another.

Before long they were joined by Chloe, Brianna and Brett's wife and daughter.

"Are you guys ready to eat yet?" Chloe asked. "We are."

"You don't need to twist *my* arm," Brett said. "There's a reason why this luau has become an annual event."

Jake got in the buffet line behind Chloe, and he soon realized that Brett had been right. The spread was incredible, and he piled his plate high.

A few families gathered together in groups to eat, but Jake, Chloe and Brianna sat alone on the blanket she'd brought from home and had spread on the lawn. When they'd eaten their fill, Brianna asked to sit with Jenny and Penny.

"Is that all right with you?" Chloe glanced at Jake as though they'd somehow become a team.

It was an interesting concept, and he nodded in agreement.

But before leaving, Brianna whispered something in Chloe's ear. Out loud she said, "Don't forget, okay?"

When she skipped off, Jake asked, "What was that all about?"

"She reminded me that the girls still want her to spend the night, and she's hoping we'll say that it's okay."

"What do you think?" he asked.

"The Townsends are a wonderful family, so Brianna will be well cared for. And she really wants to stay."

"Okay. Then if you don't mind, it's all right with me."

"Hey." Chloe cast him a heart-zapping smile. "That was our first joint decision as parents."

Yes, and as a result of that decision, the two of them would be alone for the night.

Jake suspected that Chloe had probably come to that conclusion, too, because they didn't talk much after that, which was okay. It was great just sitting outdoors with her, listening to the piped-in music and watching the flickering tiki lights that adorned the grounds.

Yet as nice as it was, the evening soon slipped away, and before he knew it, the Townsends were ready to go home and took Brianna with them.

After wishing several of the other departing neighbors a good evening, Jake and Chloe went home, where they packed a grocery bag with Brianna's pajamas and toothbrush. Then they took it to the Townsend's home and wished everyone good-night.

Brianna, who stood at the front door, clapped her hands. "This is the first time in my *whole* life that I ever had a sleepover."

Her excitement was hard to miss, and to be honest, Jake couldn't help feeling enthusiastic about the sleepover, either.

And about the chance to be alone with Chloe.

"Sleep tight, Breezy," Jake said, adopting the nickname Chloe had given her. "We'll see you bright and early in the morning."

On the way back to the condo, Chloe's shoulder brushed Jake's arm, and he had the urge to slip his hand in hers.

Instead, he decided to take it slow and easy. He'd let down his guard with her but wasn't sure how far he wanted things to go.

"Did you have fun tonight?" she asked.

"Actually, I did. Much better than I expected. I got to talk to Brett Tanner for a while. He's an interesting guy."

"Brett gets called to duty every so often, but he and Caitlin seem to have worked through it. When two people are in love, they can make any relationship work—no matter what the situation."

Was she talking about them? About their differences?

Once upon a time those differences had seemed

legion. But at this moment none of them seemed insurmountable.

Out of the corner of his eye, Jake studied Chloe as they walked toward her front porch.

The moon was only three-quarters full this evening, and it was a bright white. A cloudless sky was adorned with a splatter of twinkling stars.

But it was the stunning redhead walking next to him who'd caught his eye.

As they climbed the steps to her porch, they both reached for the doorknob at the same time. Their fingers brushed, their movements stilled and Jake's pulse kicked up a notch. He tried to repeat a mental slow-and-easy mantra, but wasn't having any luck.

Not when she turned to face him. The moment her eyes met his, their gazes locked and something wild and demanding rushed between them.

Jake wrapped her in his arms and lowered his mouth to hers.

Chapter Eleven

Jake's mouth brushed against Chloe's once, twice. On the third go-round, her lips parted and he lost it.

The kiss deepened, and his tongue swept inside her mouth, tasting, seeking.

They stood on her front porch, necking like a couple of love-struck teenagers, but Jake didn't mind. Not right now. Not when he needed to get his fill of her.

Would one kiss be enough?

He doubted it. Not when it was more than her sleek, wet mouth he wanted to explore. The urge to take her into the house, to take her to bed, was staggering.

Reason finally rallied, and they drew apart, arms still wrapped around each other, their breaths ragged with desire. He never behaved like this in public, but he'd never held this much woman before, either.

"Maybe we ought to take this indoors," he said.

"Good idea."

He turned the knob and pushed open the door. "After you."

Once inside the privacy of the cozy living room, she faced him. "I—" she cleared her throat "—I'm not very good at this sort of thing."

"You could have fooled me."

The contradiction—innocent seductress—was turning him inside out. He caught her jaw in his hand, his gaze snaring hers. "Why don't we just take things slow and easy."

Her green eyes glimmered like precious stones, and her smile, crooked with a single dimple, nearly knocked him to the floor. "Would another kiss be taking things too fast?"

A matching grin tugged at his own lips. "I don't think so."

"Good." She wrapped her arms around his neck and pulled his mouth to hers.

His control faded into the pheromone-charged room as the kiss intensified into something wild and reckless. The strength of his need ought to have scared him, but he was so caught up in desire that he didn't give a damn about anything other than this woman, this moment.

He slid his hands along the curve of her back, the slope of her bottom. A rush of heat nearly knocked him senseless, and he ran his hands along her hips, then pulled her against him.

So much for taking things slow and easy, but the increased pace, the desperation, hadn't seemed to faze her. She arched toward him and rubbed herself against his erection.

Passion flared and testosterone surged, yet common sense burst to the forefront, and he pulled back

"What's the matter?" she asked.

"I don't have any condoms." He hadn't come to California planning for their relationship to take a sexual turn.

She smiled. "I have a box, although I'm not sure whether it's outdated."

At this point he was willing to chance it. The desire to make love to her was almost overwhelming. "Where is it?"

"In my room." She took him by the hand and showed him the way, pointing to a nightstand.

She opened the drawer. Way in the back, she found a pack of condoms, never opened, never used. Apparently, Joe had been right. She wasn't as sexually active as her wardrobe had suggested.

She handed them to him, and he checked the expiration date, then set the box on the nightstand. "We're in luck. One month to spare."

He caught her cheeks in his hands, his thumbs caressing the silk of her skin, his gaze sliding deep into hers. "Are you sure about this?"

She paused as though giving it careful consideration, which was a good thing, he supposed, even if his hormones argued otherwise.

"Yes, I'm sure." Then she wrapped her arms around his neck and kissed him all over again. Yet, instead of finding any satisfaction in her kiss, his hunger for her grew tenfold.

Would he ever get his fill of this woman?

She whimpered, then threaded her fingers through his hair, drawing him closer, deeper. A moan formed low in his throat as sexual intoxication overtook him.

It might be wise to end the kiss long enough to undress, but for the life of him he couldn't stop.

As his tongue taunted hers, she pulled his shirt out of his pants, then pushed it up, revealing his stomach. She withdrew her mouth from his long enough to skim her nails over his abs. Her gaze, laden with passion, ensnared his. "I want to feel your skin against mine."

"That can be arranged." He removed his shirt and dropped it to the floor, watching as she did the same thing.

He stood transfixed, caught up in arousal, enamored by her every move as she shyly continued to peel off her pants, too.

When she stood before him in a pair of lacy white panties and a matching bra, he swallowed hard at the stunning sight before his eyes. He was afraid to breathe, afraid not to.

"You've probably heard this a million times," he

said, "but you're absolutely beautiful, Chloe. Clothes and makeup only hide your true beauty."

"Actually—" her eyes glistened with sincerity "—no one has ever said it quite like that before."

She reached behind her and unhooked her bra, releasing her breasts. He ached to touch them, to caress them. To lay claim to her body.

He bent and took a nipple in his mouth, tasting, suckling, taunting her until she cried out in pleasure.

It was all Chloe could do to hold on tight and hope her knees didn't buckle.

Jake must have sensed it because he scooped her into his arms and placed her on the bed, where he slipped off her panties and continued to stroke, caress and kiss her senseless. He began with her lips, drifting to her throat, to her breasts, to her tummy, to… Oh, my. Her breath caught as he kissed her where she'd never been kissed before. He brought her to a mountainous crest, then sent her over the edge in a brilliant, star-shattering climax.

There was no going back after tonight. And quite frankly, Chloe didn't want to. She'd never felt like this before, never ached so badly to have a man inside her.

She wanted to feel more than Jake's hands, his mouth. She wanted to make love, to feel him slide in and out, filling her and relieving the emptiness she'd lived with for as long as she could remember.

Yet she wanted to touch him, too. To taste and caress. To drive him as wild as he was driving her.

She'd had sex in the past. But this was different and so much more. Her heart was involved. And from the way Jake looked at her, the way he tried so hard to please her, she suspected he felt it, too.

He rolled to the side, taking her with him. "This is your last chance to change your mind."

She brushed a strand of hair from his forehead. What she was feeling, what he must be feeling, also, was beyond description, beyond belief. And she feared it was too good to last. But she didn't dare do anything except say, "I want you inside of me. Now."

He reached for the box on the nightstand, tore into one of the packets and protected them.

As she opened for him, he entered, and she arched up to meet him, taking all he had to offer, giving everything she had. He thrust deeply, in and out, as her body responded to his, melding, molding, until she reached a peak and cried out in release. He shuddered, climaxing along with her.

They held on tight, their heart rates rising and falling with each wave of pleasure, savoring the intimacy of what they'd shared.

She didn't know what tomorrow would bring.

But tonight, she'd been to heaven and back.

As Jake and Chloe lay amidst rumpled sheets, the scent of sex lingered in the air.

He'd never been good at the after-the-loving conversation, but this was different. He wasn't sure whether he should hold her close or roll over and bow out gracefully. He ought to say *something,* though, but he'd be damned if he could think of anything that didn't imply some kind of promise he couldn't keep.

An urge to be open and up front surfaced, suggesting he tell her all the secrets in his heart—the hurts and disappointments, the hopes and dreams—but that wasn't going to do either one of them any good.

The phone rang, drawing him from his musing. To be honest he was glad there'd been an interruption— even if it was a telemarketer or a wrong number.

Chloe sat up in bed, pulling the sheets to her chest, and reached for the receiver. "I can't imagine who that could be at this hour."

Her hair was mussed, in a sexy, after-the-loving way, reminding him of what they'd done, what he'd like to do again.

"Hello?" she said.

Jake listened to her side of the conversation, trying to decipher whether the call was important or not.

"Hi, Donna. What's the matter?" Chloe furrowed her brow, then covered the mouthpiece and spoke to Jake. "It's Brianna. She's crying and wants to come home."

"Poor kid." Jake rolled out of bed. "Tell her I'm coming. Just give me a minute or two."

As he stooped to pick up his boxers and his pants. Chloe climbed from bed, too. She was still naked.

And still breathtakingly beautiful.

While he took care of business in the bathroom,

splashed some water on his face and combed his hair, she picked up his shirt and brought it to him.

"Thanks."

"You're welcome."

He slipped on his clothes in silence.

Once their lovemaking was over, he'd begun to ponder what he ought to say, what he ought to do. And fate, it seemed, had made the decision for him, for which he ought to be glad. But he was just as uneasy as ever.

Chloe slipped on her robe, then walked him to the door. "Donna said Brianna wanted to come home because she missed her family."

Her *family?*

Or her mother?

Why hadn't he considered that she might not be ready to stay the night with people who were little more than strangers—no matter how nice they were? What if she was missing her mommy again and needing Chloe or him to hold her through it, to read to her, to keep her mind on something else?

Guilt stole over him. "Do you think we made a mistake by letting her go?"

"I don't think so." Chloe ran her fingers through her hair. "This sort of thing happens. At least, I think it does."

Something sparked in Jake's eyes, an emotion too fleeting for Chloe to get a handle on.

"We're going to make mistakes," she added. "All parents do. How could we know that the little girl begging to stay with friends would have a change of heart?"

"I didn't expect it to happen. Not when she said, 'Please, oh, *please* let me stay.' But I feel as though I've botched up my first attempt at parenthood."

Chloe placed a gentle hand on his arm. "Once, I was talking to Desiree about a woman we both knew, a single mom who moonlighted at Eddie's. She was having trouble with her kids, one of whom turned to drugs. I asked Desiree if the woman had been a good mother. And do you know what Desiree said?"

Jake shook his head.

"She said, 'Hindsight is cheap, Chloe. Any woman who puts her kids first and tries to do what she thinks is best for them at the time, right or wrong, is a good mother.'"

He hesitated momentarily, as if he were struggling with something.

"I think that goes for fathers, too."

"Maybe so."

Their gazes locked, and for a moment silence held them captive.

Then he kissed her, a heart-thumping kiss that turned her senses inside out. A hope-stirring kiss that would linger in her memory while he was gone—and longer.

As he cut across the lawn toward the Townsends' place, she closed the door and went to the bathroom. There she freshened up, then returned to the living room to greet Brianna, to welcome her home, even if they would be leaving Bayside in the morning.

Minutes later Jake carried Brianna to the house, her worn yellow blanket half draped around her. The rest dangled from his arm.

"I missed you guys too much," Brianna said, tears welling in her eyes.

"We missed you, too, Breezy."

They read her a story, and as she began to nod off, they put her to bed.

In a sense Chloe was glad the little girl was referring to her and Jake as her "family." After all, Chloe was growing to love the child more and more every day. And then there was Jake. This evening he'd touched something deep in Chloe's heart, something that had never been touched before. By anyone.

But what was going to happen if she and Jake couldn't find a way to compromise?

What if they couldn't come up with a feasible plan to create a lasting family for Brianna?

Jake thought he'd feel more settled back in Texas, more in control, yet the internal struggle remained. That push/pull he felt when it came to Chloe.

He could have ended things between them, he supposed. But something drew him to her bed each night, to her open arms. And instead of burning itself out, his desire for her only grew stronger.

On the other hand, his patience with that damn cat she'd brought home from Bayside was waning. Miss

Priss promised to be the death of him. It was enough to make a guy side with an ugly male dog who wore a pink ribbon around its neck.

As he sat at the desk in the office, trying to scan e-mail and work from the ranch, the gray tabby hissed and suddenly pounced on his leg.

"If you don't cut it out," he threatened the cat, "I'm going to call in the dog patrol. And don't let his wussy name fool you. Sweetie Pie will kick your furry butt."

Unfortunately, Miss Priss wasn't impressed.

"Ow!" he yelled, as the damn cat clawed his bare foot again—no doubt drawing blood this time. "Chloe! Brianna! Somebody come and get this cat!"

When no one responded, he swore under his breath, then searched the house until he found Chloe seated at the kitchen table, a pen in hand and her head lowered as she worked on something. A cup of coffee sat beside her.

The morning sunshine peered through the window, highlighting strands of gold in her hair and making her appear almost angelic. He couldn't help admiring her, the furrow of her brow, her parted lips.

"What are you doing?" he asked.

She looked up and smiled. "Just jotting down a few memories in my Desiree journal."

"Didn't you hear me calling you?"

Her eyes widened. "No, I didn't. I'm sorry, Jake. I get really focused when I write. What's up?"

"It's that cat. She hates me."

Chloe laughed, a soft melodious lilt that had a way of turning him every way but loose. "Maybe you should apologize to her."

"For what?"

"For not liking her in the first place." She took a sip of coffee. "And then for not even giving her a chance."

"You've got to be kidding."

She flipped through her open journal, then tapped on one of the pages. "Here it is. *Lessons from Desiree* #17: 'Give everyone a chance.' And the one just below it, #18: 'Just because someone isn't just like you doesn't mean they have less value.'"

"But Miss Priss is a cat."

"I don't think Desiree would make an issue out of that."

Deciding to take a break—okay, so he wanted some time with Chloe, with her laugh, her quick wit, her unique spin on the world—Jake poured himself a cup of coffee and took a seat next to her.

"Do you know what I think?" he asked.

"What's that?"

"That some of those lessons you're jotting down are your own."

She shrugged and smiled. "Maybe you're right. Desiree used to say that there was no shame in tripping over a crack in the sidewalk, as long as you learned to walk around it or chose to take another street the next time. You know what I mean?"

He nodded.

"I've made mistakes, and I've learned to choose different paths. So I have a few bits of wisdom to pass on to Brianna, too."

When the stunning redhead looked at him like that, her hair pulled back in a ponytail, her face nearly free of makeup and her expression real, he almost wished they could go on and on like this.

Living at the ranch.

Pretending to be a family.

But the weeks were slowly slipping away, and they would soon be faced with a major decision. And, at least on Chloe's part, a major compromise.

"Where's Brianna?" he asked.

"In her room. She's playing with the castle you gave her." Chloe lifted the mug with both hands and took a drink. "It was a good choice."

"She's really getting caught up with the princess thing."

"You've got that right. Do you know what she asked me this morning?"

"No. What?"

"She wants me to dress like a princess for her party, too. That way we can be twins."

"How are you going to talk her out of that?" he asked. "You can't very well walk into the country club dressed like Cinderella when no one else will be in costume."

"Sure I can."

Was she serious?

If Brianna got a harebrained idea and suggested Jake dress like Prince Charming, she'd be out of luck.

"Can't you talk her out of it?" he asked.

"No. I'm going to start looking for matching gowns this afternoon."

Damn. She *was* serious. "You don't have to go that far to please her."

"Jake, I'd try to turn a pumpkin into a coach, if that would make her happy and her birthday special."

He blew out a ragged sigh. "You can't give her everything she wants." Was that him who'd echoed the words his mother had once told his father?

Sometimes kids don't know what they really want or need, Gerald. So it's a parent's job to make those decisions for them. She'd been talking about his class schedule, his choice of electives.

"Don't worry," Chloe said. "I won't always give in. But Desiree wanted this birthday to be special. And besides, we promised Brianna she could plan it herself."

"Well, the invitations have to go out soon. What else does she have in mind?"

Chloe reached under her journal and withdrew a sheet of paper. "She did agree to have the party at the country club. And here's the menu she's chosen."

Jake took the paper from Chloe and read off each item. Macaroni and cheese. Hot dogs. Ice cream sundaes. Cake. And root beer. "I guess this is okay for the kids, but we'll need to have something else to offer the adults."

"Jake, this is *her* party. You shouldn't override her requests."

"There will be some of my business associates there. And they're not going to be happy with that food. There's no reason why we can't offer a buffet, with her menu included. And we'll need to offer alternate beverage selections."

"We'll do no such thing."

Jake wasn't used to being challenged. "Why not?"

"Because it's her party. And we promised to let her plan it. You're lucky she agreed to let you have your business associates on the guest list. After all, it's a child's birthday. Anyone who cares enough for her to help celebrate her special day ought to be happy to be included and shouldn't care what they eat."

"I hate macaroni and cheese. And I'm not too fond of hot dogs."

"Eat a sandwich before you go."

Damn, she was stubborn. "I'm trying to compromise, Chloe."

"And I'm not."

At this rate how were they ever going to agree upon custody and visitation?

Chloe flipped through the journal, landing on one of the first pages and rested her finger on *Lessons from Desiree* #6: "A promise is a promise. Even if it hurts."

Chapter Twelve

True to Desiree's wish, the fourteenth of July was a cotton-candy day, with big, billowy clouds that floated across a blue canvas sky.

Chloe stood at the kitchen sink and peered out the window. "Well, I'll be darned. She did it."

"Did what?" Jake asked, as he poured them each their first cup of morning coffee.

"Desiree talked to God and requested the perfect day for Brianna's party."

"You don't really believe that, do you?"

Chloe didn't respond right away. "It's not like I think she's up there trying to orchestrate things, if that's what you mean. But I know she would have prayed about it before she died. And it looks as though He honored her request for us."

She didn't come out and say that the "us" she was referring to was the three of them, but their little family, as atypical as it was, had been making some real strides in the togetherness department.

Still, Jake hadn't mentioned anything about love or the future, and she'd been afraid to broach the subject first. What if she admitted that she was falling in love with him? What if she told him she wanted to work out a way to be together, even though their interstate commutes would make that difficult?

She studied an unusual cloud formation, a fluffy swirl that looked like an ice-cream cone.

"Want me to doctor your coffee for you?" he asked.

She turned to face him. "Thanks."

While he added cream and sugar to her cup, she took a seat at the table, then waited as he served her. Not only had he misjudged *her* before they met, she'd done the same thing to him. Jake was proving to be both thoughtful and sweet.

"We'd better get a quick bite to eat," he said, "Then you'll need to get ready, especially if you girls are going in full princess regalia."

"You're right. I'll take a shower before Brianna wakes up, then do my hair."

"What are you going to do with it?" Jake asked.

The slight apprehension she picked up in his tone suggested that he feared she might dye it a rainbow of colors, but she had no intention of dressing out of the ordinary—at least, as far as princesses went.

She pulled her hair back and gave it a twist. "I thought I'd wear it up like this. What do you think?"

The tension in his expression eased. "That'll work."

For a moment, a rebellious streak reared its head. For the past few weeks, she'd been dressing casually—at least, by her standards. She'd also been going light on the makeup. And it seemed to please him, which is why she'd done it.

But she feared he wanted his friends and business associates—all of them undoubtedly as stuffy as he'd once been—to be impressed. And if it weren't for Brianna, she might backslide into the Chloe he first met. The one who boldly guarded her heart.

While they planned the party, Jake had secretly complained about almost everything Brianna had suggested, which further convinced Chloe that his friends and associates were ultraconservative and hard to please.

Chloe would try not to judge them before she met them, though. After all, like *Lessons from Desiree* #12 said: "Always give people a chance."

The one thing Jake didn't complain about was the cost of the party. He wanted Brianna's day to be every bit as special as Chloe did.

Still, they were running up quite a tally, already. By the time Chloe had purchased two blue chiffon gowns from a bridal shop and found some faux-glass slippers on eBay, one pair to fit Brianna and another for herself, she'd spent more than she had on her own wardrobe in months. And speaking of those princess shoes, Chloe might look like Cinderella on the outside, but with her toes all scrunched up, she was going to feel like one of the wicked stepsisters at the party.

Still, she didn't mind. Not if it made Brianna happy.

"You should have seen the look on her face when the package arrived with the wands and tiaras in them," Chloe said.

"I'm glad this is coming together so well." Jake took another drink of his coffee, then fingered the mug. "And I appreciate you talking her into adding a few other entrees to the menu. How'd you do that?"

Chloe grinned. "I gave your concerns some thought, then mentioned to her that we probably ought to have some traditional castle food, too. When she agreed, I suggested chicken à la king. That sounded like a good idea to her. So did His Majesty's salmon and the royal prime rib of beef."

"Clever." Jake smiled. "Thanks for helping me out."

"You're welcome." Chloe got up from the table and carried her cup to the sink, where she rinsed it and placed it upside down in the top rack of the dishwasher. "She also wanted to add porridge as another option, but I talked her out of that. So you owe me."

"You're right. Thanks." Jake lifted his mug and finished his coffee. At first he'd considered Chloe his parental nemesis, but he was beginning to realize she was on his side. She just had a unique way about providing her support. She also had an incredible desire to remain independent and free-spirited.

He could live with that. Couldn't he?

Two hours later, after a slew of muffled giggles and undoubtedly a lot of fuss, Chloe escorted Brianna out of the bedroom and into the living room.

Jake had been keeping an eye on the clock over the mantel. He might have been seated in an easy chair, but he was nowhere near relaxed. In fact, he'd intended to herd Brianna and Chloe into the car the minute they appeared. Instead, when he spotted them, he'd jumped up, then stopped dead in his tracks.

Their hair swept up into mounds of curls, Brianna and Chloe walked into the room wearing matching outfits—blue Cinderella gowns, rhinestone tiaras and…shoes that looked like glass slippers. They carried scepters. Or maybe they were magic wands.

Either way, he couldn't quell the grin that broke out on his face. "Well, I'll be darned. I've never been in the company of royalty before. Now I wish I'd worn a tuxedo."

"We'll wait," Brianna said, "if you want to change."

"Oh, no, Your Highness. It's too late to do that. Our coach is waiting."

The child's eyes widened. "Our *coach?*"

Jake led them to the entry, then opened the front door and stood aside. As Brianna peered into the yard and spotted the sleek, white limousine Jake had hired, she gasped in delight.

"I'm afraid it's not pumpkin season yet," Jake said, "so I could only manage this."

The driver, a dapper, silver-haired gentleman in a black suit, stood near the open passenger door, his hands clasped behind his back.

"Go on," Jake told his little sister. "Get inside. We don't want to be late to the ball."

Brianna giggled, then climbed into the back of the limousine.

Chloe took Jake by the arm and turned him to her. Her smile and a teary glimmer in her eyes nearly knocked him to his knees. "This was a lovely touch. For a while, I'd thought you were the birthday grinch, but see? You really can let loose and have fun. I'm proud of you."

Something warm and bright pierced his chest, causing his heart to swell. "Thanks, but keep in mind that I'm still not wearing a costume."

"Actually," she said, "I'm a bit disappointed. I really adore men in tights."

"Too bad. You're stuck with me."

She brushed a kiss across his lips. "Actually, I'm kind of stuck *on* you."

Jake stood in silence as Chloe carefully wrestled the skirt of her gown so she could climb in the limo with Princess Brianna.

For a moment he wanted to quiz her, to see how far she'd go to explain what she'd meant by being stuck on him. But then that might lead to the subject they'd been avoiding since the first time they'd made love.

The "Now what?" that had been riding on the tip of his tongue.

And truthfully? He didn't know. Instead, he waited for her to slide into the limousine, letting the comment go untouched.

The birthday party had been a hit with adults and children alike. Even though Brianna's California friends, Jenny and Penny, hadn't been able to attend, she was happy to share her day with the kids from the playgroup she and her mother had once been a part of in the nearby community of Granger.

And surprisingly, even some of the conservative friends and colleagues Jake had included on the guest list, along with their children, had complimented him on the theme. Most of them passed on the root beer, though, and slipped off to the bar for a bigger beverage selection.

But they'd all been especially charmed by Chloe, who'd taken on the role of the queen mother all day long. The lovely redhead was a great actress, especially when in costume. And in spite of it all, her focus was on Brianna during the festivities, like any good mama, and she took a ton of pictures.

And speaking of mothers, Jake's had been noticeably absent, even though she'd been invited.

He'd always understood why she wouldn't want to be close to her ex-husband's child by another woman, but why now? Poor little Brianna had been orphaned and Jake was going to be raising her. Making a home for her at his town house in Dallas.

Besides, Brianna was as cute and sweet as a little girl could be. Who wouldn't adore her?

So, no, he wasn't buying into his mother's last-minute, feigned headache. What would it have hurt her to have at least made an appearance?

He'd always tried to put himself in his mom's place, to understand where she was coming from. Yet she'd never seemed to give him the same courtesy.

Still, ever since he'd been a boy, he'd wanted to connect with the woman who'd given birth to him, the woman who'd sold him out for a bigger divorce settlement.

So what made him think anything had changed now?

Maybe it was time to let go. To quit trying.

They returned to the ranch in the limousine at four-thirty and unloaded all the gifts. Mrs. Davies, who had weekends off, had stayed in Dallas after the party. So Chloe had made chicken-noodle soup and turkey sandwiches for dinner.

Now Jake sat on a recliner in the family room, watching television while Chloe read a bedtime story to Brianna.

He held the remote, scanning the stations until he found an action flick he'd already seen. Still, the plot was intriguing and the special effects were great.

When his cell rang, he turned down the volume on

the TV, then pulled the phone from the clip on his belt and answered.

"Mr. Braddock," a female voice said, "this is Helen Walters from Raleigh Academy."

Jake settled back into the chair. "Yes, Helen. What can I do for you?"

"I'm calling to let you know that Brianna's application has been reviewed and we're now ready to take the next step in our enrollment process. I'd like to schedule the home visitation. I'd also like to set up a day for a readiness test, which we hold on our campus on Saturday mornings."

"All right," Jake said, heading to the office to check his calendar.

"I know this is short notice, but we have another student who lives fairly close to Granger, so we were hoping we could schedule you both on the same day."

"Of course." The computer was up and running, so Jake quickly opened up his calendar for the month.

"The trouble is," Mrs. Walters said, "the other child and his parents will be heading to Europe for their three-week vacation, and tomorrow afternoon is the only time the family will be available."

Tomorrow? Jake had been expecting the call, but not this soon. He'd planned to send Chloe shopping or on an errand while the school reps came to visit, but now he was backed into a corner.

Of course, he had to admit that Chloe had done well at the country club today, handling herself with grace and charm. Even his own mother would have been hard-pressed to fault her, if she'd actually shown up.

And Chloe hadn't been hiding behind her wardrobe, any longer.

Why was he even stressing over this? Chloe would do fine. "Tomorrow evening will work for us, Mrs. Walters. What time did you have in mind?"

"How about five o'clock? We won't be staying long. We should be gone before the dinner hour."

"Okay, we'll see you then."

When the line disconnected, Jake remained in the office, seated in his father's swivel chair. He would need to choose his words carefully, to plot a strategy. Chloe wasn't the kind of woman who could be easily persuaded to do anything she didn't want to do.

From the first night they'd made love and each time since, they'd tiptoed around the future, around the upcoming decision to be made, the sacrifices they each expected the other to make.

To tell the truth, Jake was beginning to like having Chloe around—in his life, in his bed. They made a good team, both sexually and now as parents.

She'd come a long way since he'd first met her.

In fact, they were due back at the attorney's office on Thursday morning. Maybe by the time the two of them drove to Dallas for the meeting, Jake could convince her to see reason and remain in Texas longer.

After all, she enjoyed living in the city. At least,

that's the impression he had. So why not make her primary residence in Dallas and fly back to California on occasion to check on her property and holdings?

It's not like he would jump into anything like marriage, so it didn't have to be a permanent arrangement. They could take one day at a time.

At the sound of footsteps padding down the hall, Jake looked up and saw Chloe. She made a circle with her index finger and thumb, indicating everything was A-okay.

"Is Brianna asleep?" he asked.

Chloe nodded. "She was exhausted."

"Hey, birthdays will do that to you. And if you have enough of them, they really begin to wear on you."

"Cute." She smiled. "You know, there was a time when I didn't think you had a sense of humor."

He shrugged. "I think we both misjudged each other."

She leaned against the door frame, her hair hanging softly down her back in a cascade of curls, her feet bare. "What are you doing in here? I thought you'd gotten caught up on your work earlier today."

"I just had a call."

She didn't ask, but he figured she was curious.

"Remember the school I was talking to you about? Raleigh Academy?"

She crossed her arms, her expression going from casual to apprehensive. "Yes."

"Well, I've scheduled a home visitation, and they'll be coming tomorrow around five o'clock."

She didn't speak right away. And for a moment she didn't even move. Then she straightened like a tin soldier on alert.

"I know it's a little late in the day," Jake said, "but they won't stay long."

Silence hovered over them, and tension stretched between them like a frayed bungee cord that had seen better days.

When she finally spoke, she said, "I thought we were a team, Jake."

"We *are*."

"Then why didn't you ask me how I felt about her going to a private school?"

"I thought I did." He turned his seat so that he faced her.

"You mentioned it to Dr. Rodgers, and I clearly stated that I didn't want her to go to a private school. That there were plenty of good schools, *even* in California."

"I realize we haven't exactly come to a conclusion about where she'll be living—"

"You're absolutely right. We *haven't*. So why in the world did you assume you could make a unilateral decision about her education without discussing it with me? You knew I was opposed to Raleigh Academy."

"You haven't even seen it."

"I don't need to." She cinched her arms tighter.

"It's just a little visit. That's all. It doesn't mean she has to attend Raleigh in the fall. It just ensures

JUDY DUARTE   219

that we could make that choice if we want to. Wasn't
that one of Desiree's lessons? 'Never limit your options'?"

"As a matter of fact, you're right. That's number
fourteen."

Jake got out of his chair and eased closer. "You
and I haven't decided where she'll go to school, of
course, but if she does attend Raleigh, her application needs to be approved by the end of this month.
And in order for that to happen, the committee needs
to visit her home and meet her family. They'll also
need to schedule a readiness exam."

"Why didn't you tell me about this ahead of
time?" She drew back from him, stepping into the
hall. "This is the kind of thing parents need to discuss
with each other."

"You're right. I'm sorry. I should have talked to
you about it first." At least Jake had the rest of the
night and most of the day to get her to see things
his way. It wouldn't do for Chloe to get her hackles
raised before the visit. Especially now that she knew
it had been scheduled.

The way he figured it, getting her to see things his
way shouldn't be too tough.

But when Chloe turned and headed back to the
bedroom, snapping the door shut behind her, he suddenly wasn't so sure.

Last night it had taken all Chloe had not to slam
the bedroom door when she'd retreated from the office

to lick her wounds. Memories of her days at Preston Prep had flipped through her mind like frames on an old nickelodeon: Chloe walking the school halls all alone because no one wanted to be seen with her; the lies about her written in various shades of indelible ink on the walls of the bathroom stalls; the whispers that went on behind her back; the snickers.

Some kids could be *so* cruel. And their petty remarks could scar others for life. Chloe didn't want Brianna subjected to even a fraction of what she'd been through as a child.

How could Jake go behind Chloe's back and enroll Brianna in a school without discussing it with her?

He was assuming that Chloe would either yield custody to him—which she wouldn't do—or else he figured that the third party would naturally conclude that he was the better parent.

And to top it off, he'd had the nerve to quote Desiree in his defense, going so far as to take her words out of context.

Never limit your options, he'd said. *Isn't that one of Desiree's lessons?*

Yes, it was Lesson #14. But last night, Chloe hadn't pointed out *Lessons from Desiree* #15: "Never underestimate your opponents."

Later, after Chloe had showered and gotten ready for bed, Jake had knocked lightly on her bedroom, but she'd failed to respond. She'd expected him to go on his way, but instead he'd slipped into her room and climbed into her bed.

She'd feigned sleep, rolling to the side and facing the wall.

The next morning he'd apologized, and she'd implied that she'd forgiven him, although she hadn't.

For the rest of the day she'd remained fairly quiet, a game plan swirling around in her mind.

And now, as it neared four o'clock in the afternoon, she decided it was time to put her plan into action.

"They'll be here soon," Jake said.

"I suppose I'd better go change my clothes."

"That white dress you wore while shopping in Bayside would look good. Or the black one you wore to the meeting with the redevelopment council."

Chloe couldn't believe how foolish she'd been, falling in love with a man who would try to change everything about her…if she'd let him. A man who would try to control her every move. "Don't worry, Jake. I know what you expect of me."

That, of course, didn't mean she would follow orders, implied or otherwise.

She was just putting the finishing touches on her makeup when she took a good, hard look at the woman in the mirror. Yesterday, Cinderella had peered back at her. Today? One of the wicked stepsisters.

For a moment, she reconsidered how Jake would react to her rebellion and had second thoughts.

But not for long. Jake had completely disregarded her opinion and her wishes when he'd set up the visit with the school representatives, and her memories of her days at Preston Prep tumbled to the forefront of her mind. As horrid as they all had been, one stood out from the rest.

She'd been in the seventh grade.

When it had become clear that her classmates weren't going to accept her and would shun any child who'd tried to be her friend, Chloe had focused on academics. And one day her hard work paid off. During an all-school assembly in the gym, Chloe's name had been announced as the student of the month.

She'd been thrilled, until a collective groan had sounded from the stands. She'd tried to hold her head up high, proud to have finally achieved some sort of recognition at school, yet having it all sullied by the reaction of her peers.

But it hadn't stopped there. Later in the day, she'd found a rolled-up page from a *Playboy* magazine stuck in her backpack, a black circle drawn around a redheaded playmate of the month.

"Practice makes perfect" was sketched across the top.

Even now, the pain was still fresh, raw. The tears still close to the surface.

When the doorbell rang, letting Chloe know the visitors had arrived, she leaned forward, brushed on another thick coat of mascara, then applied a dark shade of red lipstick called Hot Mama.

Next she slipped into the skimpy black dress she'd worn to the attorney's office six weeks ago, when she'd met with Jake to discuss the requirements of

Desiree's will. After she'd shimmied into the form-fitting dress, she studied herself in the mirror.

Not bad.

Just yesterday she'd donned glass slippers and a Cinderella gown. And today she wore stiletto heels and a tight, black knit dress with a thigh-high hem. Both times there'd been a reason for her efforts. A very good one.

Now all she had to do was ruffle the feathers of the fine folks from Raleigh Academy, and Jake would be forced to consider other schools. Places where a kid could be herself and not be forced to conform to standards set beyond her reach.

As Chloe strode into the living room, she spotted a matronly woman with graying hair dressed in a black business suit. A slight, bald man wearing a blue sports jacket and brown slacks stood at her side.

Jake turned first, his bright-eyed smile drooping into a frown the moment Chloe entered. If looks could kill, she would have just taken her last breath.

In fact, for a moment, as she spotted the disappointment in Jake's eyes, her resolve waffled. But she'd made a decision and set the ball in motion; she couldn't very well backpedal now.

"Hello, everyone." She lifted her hand and wiggled her fingers, the silver bangle bracelets on her arm clinking together. "My name is Chloe. I'm sure Jake has told you all about me and my unshakeable faith in the public school system."

"I'm Helen Walters," the woman said, struggling

to keep a generic expression on her face and failing miserably. "I'm the principal of Raleigh Academy."

"It's nice to meet you, Helen." Chloe turned to the man, who stood and adjusted his glasses on the bridge of his nose. "Hello, there."

"Arnold Robertson," he said, extending his hand.

Chloe grasped it in both of hers. "It's nice to meet you, Arnie."

"Well, I, uh——" he glanced at Helen Walters, then cleared his throat "——I haven't been called Arnie in a very long time."

Jake shot her a knock-that-off-this-instant glare, then morphed into superhost. "Why don't we all have a seat." With his right arm, he indicated the cream-colored leather sofa and matching love seat.

Chloe chose the spot next to Arnie.

"How are you related to Brianna?" Mrs. Walters asked Chloe.

"I'm her guardian."

"Only until Thursday," Jake interjected. The intensity of his gaze was enough to laser an escape hole in the wall behind Chloe.

But she wasn't going anywhere. Nor would she back down. "Custody is still yet to be determined, isn't it?"

Helen cleared her throat, then scanned the room. "Where is little Brianna? We'd like to meet her, too."

"Of course," Jake said. "I'll get her."

When he left, Helen turned to Chloe and forced a smile. "So, tell us a bit about you, Ms. Haskell."

Chloe crossed one leg over the top of the other,

tugging the stretchy material back where it belonged. "There's not much to tell. I'm from California, where I own a small dance place in the inner city. It's not nearly as lucrative as my father's business was, though."

"Your father is a businessman?" Helen asked.

"*Was*," Chloe corrected. "Before he died, he owned Eddie's Place, which was a bar and strip club not far from the Rescue Mission. It was very success-ful, especially on Friday and Saturday nights."

Talk about Kodak moments. The look the two com-mittee members passed to each other was priceless.

Before either of them could recover, Jake re-turned to the living room with Brianna, introducing her to the group.

A stab of indecision and remorse pricked Chloe's heart, yet she shook it off. She'd rather die of embar-rassment or regret than see Brianna suffer any of what she'd gone through. And even if the children were good to Brianna, accepting of her, what if their snobbish attitudes rubbed off on her? What if she be-came the kind of little rich girl who would be cruel to someone she deemed different than her?

Helen leaned forward. "Well, hello, young lady. You must be Brianna. My friend, Mr. Robertson, and I came all the way out to Granger to meet you."

Brianna nodded then made her way to Chloe. "You should see my castle. I have it all fixed up with the little people you gave me for my birthday."

"I can't wait to see it, Breezy."

Brianna smiled. "How come your lipstick is so red?"

"Just because." Chloe wasn't as eager to put on the act with Brianna around. If the little girl truly wanted to go to Raleigh Academy, if she had friends there, if…

Oh, dear God. Had her own emotions, her own memories clouded her judgment? Had she made a mistake she might regret?

"Isn't Chloe pretty?" Brianna asked.

"She *can* be," Jake said.

The truth, the weight of what she'd done, slammed into her, and she didn't feel the least bit pretty now.

Brianna leaned into Chloe. "I want to be just like you when I grow up."

"Is that so?" Mrs. Walters asked.

Arnie glanced at his wristwatch. "Well, Helen, we probably ought to be going. We wouldn't want to interrupt the Braddocks' dinner routine."

"No, we wouldn't," Helen said, getting to her feet. She extended a hand to Jake. "It was very nice meeting you. We'll be in touch."

"Thank you for coming." Jake stood.

As he showed them the door, Chloe leaned back in her seat. She'd done it. She'd undermined the interview.

Trouble was, she didn't feel particularly pleased at having done so.

At least Brianna wouldn't have to go through the tears and angst Chloe had suffered when she'd been a child. Nor would she grow up to inflict that kind of pain on someone else.

The downside, she feared, was that Jake might

never forgive her. And the cost suddenly seemed overwhelming.

When Jake finally returned to the living room, Chloe suspected he was only holding on to his temper by a frayed thread. "Brianna, would you please go into your room and play for a while? I need to talk to Chloe alone."

"Okay."

As the child dashed off, he placed one hand on his hip and pointed at her with the index finger of the other. "You did that on purpose. You blew Brianna's chances to attend one of the finest schools in Texas."

"No, I blew your efforts to orchestrate a decision without consulting me."

He combed a hand through his hair. "I tried to do some damage control outside with Mrs. Walters and Mr. Roberson, but I'm afraid it's over."

Chloe hoped so.

"And I'm not just talking about the visitation and Brianna's acceptance at Raleigh Academy. This entire six-week experiment has been a joke. To think I trusted you. That I thought…I hoped…" He swore under his breath. "I believed you and I could work out some kind of compromise, some kind of…"

He didn't continue, and she didn't press him for more.

How could she when she knew he was right?

Chapter Thirteen

Jake had been furious after the committee left the house, but he'd refrained from saying anything in front of Brianna, which hadn't been easy. He'd been about to blow sky-high.

How could Chloe have done that to me? he'd asked himself over and over. He'd let down his guard, trusted her. Believed that she'd changed. Believed that they'd actually shared something beyond Brianna, beyond sex.

She knew how to make a good impression when she wanted to, but for some reason, she'd been determined to screw things up. To what lengths would she go to fight Jake on other issues, especially on custody of Brianna?

He'd underestimated her, but he wouldn't do so again.

Whatever had possessed him to even think that the two of them could come up with any kind of compromise?

Brianna's chances of attending Raleigh Academy were slim to none. And now he'd have to scramble to find an alternate school for her to attend.

He'd slept fitfully that night after Chloe had sabotaged the visitation. And the next morning, before Mrs. Davies arrived to start her week, Jake found Chloe in the kitchen.

She'd showered and was wearing a robe as she stood by the coffeemaker, but she seemed subdued.

Was she feeling guilty? he wondered. Or just smug and self-assured?

After pouring herself a cup of coffee, she turned. Her hair had been pulled back into a ponytail, and she wore no makeup. Neither had she tried to mask the dark circles under her eyes.

He almost weakened, almost asked her to sit down and discuss some sort of compromise. Instead he asked, "How much money would it take for you to just bow out and let me raise my sister alone?"

Something flickered in her eyes. He wished he could say it was a flash of greed. An indication that she would agree to his terms. But he feared it was something else. Something that had struck a blow.

That was good, wasn't it? That she felt remorse about what she'd done?

She placed her mug on the countertop and crossed her arms. "My love can't be bought or sold, Jake, although your offer makes me suspect that yours can. So for that reason, I'm willing to offer you the same terms. I have a checkbook, too."

Jakes' gut clenched, as her words hit their mark. To be honest, there was a part of him that was glad she'd refused his money. And another part that was sorry he couldn't find a way out of this sorry mess.

Rather than respond to her counteroffer, he strode to the service porch and reached for his hat, intent on saddling up one of the horses and escaping into the countryside. He did some of his best thinking while riding the hills on horseback, but something told him he wouldn't be able to think himself out of this situation.

And he'd been right. Two hours later not one option had come to mind. Nor had one cropped up after he cooled down his horse and put it away.

As a result he and Chloe finished out the last few days together, fulfilling the agreement they'd made at Brian Willoughby's office six weeks earlier but barely talking to each other. What was the point?

At one o'clock on Thursday afternoon, they returned to the attorney's office.

They'd left Brianna with Mrs. Davies at the ranch, where the poor kid had no clue that her life, her fate, now lay in the hands of a third party.

"Come on back," Willoughby said, as he led them to a small conference room, where they both took a seat.

Chloe had dressed conservatively today—imagine that. Yet she'd also lost her effervescence, her smile, her zest for life—something Jake missed.

"Have you reached an agreement?" the attorney asked.

Jake glanced at Chloe, caught her gaze, which acknowledged the truth. He returned his focus to Willoughby. "I'm afraid not."

"That's too bad. I'm sorry to hear it." Willoughby leaned back in his chair. "I'll set up a meeting at the ranch with the designated third party this evening. I've got several appointments after this one, but I'll drive out when I'm done. Will six o'clock be all right?"

It would have to be. The sooner they could get on with their lives, the better for everyone.

"Do you mind telling us who the third party is?" Jake asked.

"Not just yet." Willoughby clasped his hands on the desktop. "I'm just following Desiree's instructions to the letter."

"I understand." Jake stood and turned to Chloe. "Are you ready?"

She nodded, then stood, too.

They returned to the ranch in silence, but that didn't mean Jake's mind wasn't going a mile a minute.

Willoughby had said, *I'll drive out to the ranch.*

If he'd been planning to bring someone with him, wouldn't he have used the word *we?*

Of course, the third party could be driving out in

a separate car. But Jake began to suspect the ultimate judge was already at the ranch.

He swore under his breath for not considering it all along.

Mrs. Davies had been given a three-year contract prior to Desiree's death. And who better to make a judgment about Brianna's best interests than the woman who'd lived on the ranch each Monday through Friday for the past six weeks? Who else had observed both Chloe's and Jake's interactions with the child?

An uneasiness stole over him. He'd been friendly with Mrs. Davies, but not any more than he was with any other of his employees.

Would that hurt his chances?

Damn. He'd turned on the charm with the psychologist, but maybe he should have been more concerned about schmoozing with the housekeeper.

Yet guilt overrode regret.

He didn't know squat about Mrs. Davies, a woman who'd made sure the household ran smoothly, a woman who'd poured her heart and soul into the meals she'd prepared. All he knew was that she was a nice lady and a fabulous cook.

But where did she go on weekends? What did she do with her free time?

A journal entry he'd seen while Chloe had pointed out another came to mind. *Lessons from Desiree* #9: "Everyone has value. All you need to do is look for it."

Double damn.

Now *he* was starting to quote Desiree.

And…was learning from her.

Chloe had stared out the window of Jake's SUV all the way from Dallas to the ranch, studying the countryside, her heart aching with all she stood to lose.

Several times she turned to speak to Jake, to tell him she was sorry, but she wasn't entirely sure what she was sorry for.

When they entered the house through the service porch, they found Brianna and Mrs. Davies baking chocolate-chip cookies.

Brianna, her eyes bright, had no idea what the immediate future would bring. No clue that life as she'd just gotten to know it was going to change all over again.

"Want to see what we're going to have for dessert tonight?" the little girl asked.

"Oh, look. Cookies." Chloe forced a smile. "I'll bet they're going to be yummy."

"Now that you're home, I'll take a little break." Mrs. Davies wiped her hands on a dish towel. "I need to give one of my sisters a call. She's been feeling under the weather lately."

"I'm sorry to hear that," Jake said. "How many sisters do you have, Mrs. Davies?"

"Three. Sheri is the baby, the one I've always been closest to."

Jake reached for a cookie. "Where does she live?"

"Texarkana. But don't worry about the cost of the call. I'll use my cell."

"Don't be silly," Jake said. "I don't care about the phone bill. It's just that I realized I didn't know very much about you. About the things and people that matter to you. And I'm sorry that I never took time to ask."

"Well, there's not much to tell. I'm a widow and have two children, Phillip and Natalie. They're both off at college."

"You must be proud," Jake said.

The woman beamed. "I certainly am."

"Well, I won't keep you. It's just that I realized both my father and stepmother thought highly of you. And I'm sure it went beyond the fact that you're an exceptional cook."

"Well, thank you."

Jake shrugged, then reached for a second cookie from the platter that sat on the table.

"By the way," Mrs. Davies said, as she paused near the back door. "The teapot is on the counter."

"The teapot?" Chloe asked.

"Yes." Mrs. Davies pointed to the child-sized china pot that rested next to several little cups and saucers. "Brianna wanted to have a tea party, and I assumed…well, it seemed like the kind of thing you would agree to do with her."

"Will you?" Brianna asked. "Will you put on your princess gown and have tea with me?"

"Of course."

"And you, too, Jake. You don't have to wear your tuxedo. Just be with us and pretend, okay?"

Chloe expected him to balk. Instead, he slid his little sister a grin. "Sure, Breezy. I'll join you."

Five minutes later Chloe returned from her room wearing the blue chiffon gown. She hoped Breezy didn't expect her to wear those darn glass slippers. She was still nursing blisters from the last time she'd worn them.

"We're in here," the child called from her room.

When Chloe entered the pink-walled bedroom, she found Brianna wearing her own Cinderella dress and playing hostess to Jake, who sat scrunched in a small chair, his knees bent awkwardly.

She couldn't help but grin at the sight, yet a bittersweet whisper swept through her, taunting her with a vision of what might have been.

"You can sit here." Brianna pulled out a little chair, and Chloe took a seat next to Jake.

They shared sweetened, lukewarm tea from the little china pot. As they went through the motions of a tea party fit for royalty, Chloe's heart was so heavy, she feared it would drop to the bottom of her feet.

But Jake, too, appeared somber. Forcing a smile.

Was he worried about the decision that would be made? Fearing that custody might be awarded to Chloe? Or was he concerned about the upheaval Brianna would soon face.

Chloe wanted to hate him, to blame him. But how

could she remain angry at a man who adored his little sister and only wanted what was best for her? A man who'd at least thought he was ensuring a better future for her by considering a private education?

As much as his words had hurt, he'd been right. Chloe had sabotaged what he was trying to do. And although the two of them stood no chance of ever becoming romantically involved again, it didn't mean she didn't care for him. That she didn't love him.

He was a stubborn and stuffy Texan. And she was a fool for getting involved with the wrong man again. Jake would make her life miserable if they ever decided to live in the same house. But there was nothing she could do about her feelings.

Lessons from Desiree #16: "We don't choose love; it chooses us."

"You know what?" Brianna said, placing one hand on Jake and the other on Chloe.

"What's that?" Jake asked.

"I love my family. And even if Mommy and Daddy can't be here with me, I'm glad you are."

Chloe's eyes filled with tears, but not the happy kind. The kind that threatened to tear her heart in two.

There was no way she could put that child through any more pain or disappointment than necessary. And she'd be darned if she'd drag her off and make her live in Bayside, when she could at least have this house, this room, remain just as she remembered it.

"I hate to interrupt," Mrs. Davies said from the bedroom doorway. "But, I just sat down to place my call when Sweetie Pie ran off with my reading glasses. And he's climbed under the bed in the spare room. I'm afraid he won't listen to me, and I was wondering if Brianna would coax him out."

"Don't worry, Mrs. Davies." Brianna kicked off her glass slippers. "Sweetie Pie is only playing with you. I'll tell him to give you the glasses back."

As the little girl dashed off, Mrs. Davies on her heels, Chloe reached over and placed her hand on Jake's arm.

"I'm sorry for screwing up the interview." A tear slid down her cheek, then another. "It's just that I went to a school that was so exclusive, so snobbish, that my life was miserable for years. And I hadn't wanted Brianna to go through the same thing. I should have shared the reason for my apprehension about her going to Raleigh Academy. I didn't want to risk seeing her go through anything as painful, and I didn't trust you to listen, let alone understand."

Jake nodded. "And I should have discussed the school thing with you first. I'm so used to making things happen on the job that I got carried away. We were supposed to be coparenting, and I dropped the ball on that."

"I know we already met with Mr. Willoughby and told him we couldn't come to an agreement, but that's no longer true. I couldn't love Brianna any more if I'd given birth to her, and I don't want to see her suffer any more losses, any more changes in her life." Another tear slipped down Chloe's cheek, and she brushed it away. "Desiree made the ultimate sacrifice by trying to transition Brianna into a new life without a mother. And I won't do anything less. You keep her with you. Just promise me you'll bring her to the ranch on weekends. And that you'll let her visit me during the summers."

Jake reached out and cupped Chloe's cheek, his thumb brushing away the tears.

Chloe was giving up Brianna, yet Jake didn't feel like he'd won anything.

How much will it take for you to bow out of her life? he'd asked her. And the answer was: a broken heart.

Jake remembered how his father had bought off his mother and realized he was guilty of the same thing with Chloe.

"I know you hate being out on the ranch," Chloe said. "But promise me you'll bring her out here regularly. Every weekend, if you can manage it."

The same routine his father had insisted upon.

But it wasn't true that Jake had hated the ranch. He'd actually liked a lot of the same things his father had—ranching and playing cowboy on the weekends. But he'd tried so hard to convince his mother of his worth, of his value, that he'd begun to shun the things he had in common with his father.

So he'd let her "smooth his rough edges," something he was just now beginning to realize he'd allowed. Something he was ashamed to admit.

Yet his father had known it all along.

And so had Desiree.

"For what it's worth," Jake said, "I've actually enjoyed the time I spent here with you and Brianna. Coming out to the ranch on weekends won't be a big sacrifice."

Yet it wouldn't be the same with Chloe gone. In a sense, he was losing something in the bargain they'd struck. Something more valuable than he'd realized.

And Brianna was losing, too. His little sister had the opportunity to have a mother again—in Chloe.

"I'm not sure that we've reached the compromise Desiree had been hoping for." Jake stroked his knuckles along Chloe's cheek, felt the dampness, the softness of her skin. "Look at you. What kid wouldn't thank her lucky stars each night to know she had a princess for a mom."

Chloe's tears began anew. "You have no idea how much I appreciate hearing you say that."

"Yeah, well, I mean it. And for that reason I'll give up Brianna to you with the same terms. Liberal visitation during the summer."

"Somehow I don't think that's what Desiree had wanted, either."

They'd never know for sure, Jake supposed.

It would be tough not having Brianna around. But it wasn't just his sister he hated to give up. He'd gotten attached to Chloe, too.

She had a loving heart and a creative flair. Something he was going to miss like hell.

But how could two opposites who lived in separate states raise a child together and create a family?

* * *

The attorney arrived at six o'clock, but he came alone. And when he asked to speak to Jake, Chloe and Brianna in private, Mrs. Davies headed to her room in the guesthouse for the evening.

"Where's the third party?" Jake asked.

"She's already here," Brian Willoughby said. "Desiree had asked that Brianna make the final decision. So, let's all go and sit down where we can be more comfortable."

The man took Brianna by the hand and led her into the living room.

Jake grabbed Chloe's arm, slowing her movement, then whispered, "That's an awful lot to dump on a child."

"I'm sure that's why Desiree had hoped we'd come to an agreement, ourselves."

Jake mumbled something under his breath, then cupped his hand over his mouth so only Chloe would hear. "Desiree should have realized that we both have ties in separate states. And that we… Well, what did she expect?"

"I'm not sure, but my guess is that she hoped you and I would fall in love, and that we'd all live at the ranch as one big happy family."

Jake slowly shook his head. Desiree might have suspected that something romantic could grow between him and Chloe, but not if they couldn't compromise. Not if they couldn't put the other's best interests above their own.

And not when those interests were miles apart.

"Living together on the ranch is impossible," he said, although he couldn't help searching Chloe's eyes, looking for some kind of argument.

"I know." Her words came out softly, but not because it was meant to be a whisper. It was more of an acceptance of fact.

"I won't let him do this to her," Jake said. "We can't ask her to choose one of us. We need to settle this between ourselves."

"I've already agreed to give her up."

"But do you think that's in her best interests?"

"It's certainly not in mine."

"Then stay in Texas," he said. "We can live together here at the ranch."

What he was proposing was tempting, but he wasn't *proposing* the right thing. Chloe had come to love Jake. Come to hope for more than a child-rearing arrangement between coparents who happened to sleep with each other on occasion.

"No, Jake. It's not enough."

"What do you mean?"

"I'm not sure how it happened. Nor why it did. And Heaven knows I never expected it. But I've fallen in love with you, and living together isn't enough."

"What more do you want?" he asked.

"You figure it out." Then she turned on her heel and joined the attorney and Brianna in the living room.

Her heart was ready to break in a million tiny

pieces, but she couldn't sell herself short. Not even for Desiree.

Once they'd all taken their seats, Mr. Willoughby turned to Brianna. "Sweetheart, I have to talk to you about something."

She looked first at Jake, then Chloe. "What about?"

"You know that Jake has a house in Dallas, which is a long drive from here."

She nodded.

"And Chloe has a house in Bayside, which is even farther away."

Brianna nodded again. "We have to take an airplane to go there."

"That's right. And since they both love you very much, they'd like you to decide which house you want to live in."

Brianna smiled broadly. "I want to live *here*. In *my* house. With my *family*."

"But Chloe and Jake have work to do, businesses to maintain."

"Then I can stay here with Mrs. Davies while they go to work. And they can come home and be with me at night. That's what families do."

"She's right," Jake said. "They find a way to compromise. And if they love one another, they fulfill their commitments, even if it hurts."

"So what are you saying?" Willoughby asked.

"That I'm willing to agree to the wishes of the will of the princess I've recently come to love."

"Me?" Brianna asked.

"Oh," Jake said, "but I've *always* loved you, Your Highness. It's Princess Chloe that I've just fallen in love with."

The look on Chloe's face was priceless. "You love me?"

"I've fought my feelings for you, denied them. And when that failed, I ignored them and told myself we were too different, that we didn't want the same things out of life. But I don't believe that's true." Jake stood and made his way to the chair where Chloe sat, then knelt before her and took her hand in his. "But the truth is that I've fallen head-over-heart in love with you, honey. And I want us to be the family Desiree hoped we'd be. In Bayside, in Dallas and here at the ranch."

Chloe's heart filled to the brim, and the tears began all over again. But this time they were from unadulterated joy.

"I love you, too." She wrapped her arms around him and held him tight. "I have no idea how we'll work out the logistics, but I know we will."

Then she kissed him long and deep, her hopes and dreams mingling with his.

Mr. Willoughby cleared his throat. "You have no idea how happy I am that you came to that conclusion."

"Why is that?" Jake asked.

"Because Desiree swore up and down that you two would fall in love—given the chance. And that you both would put Brianna's best interests above your own. Quite frankly, I was afraid she'd been wrong.

And I just hated having to come over here tonight and put Brianna in the position of having to choose."

"Well, Desiree was right all along," Jake said.

"Where's my journal?" Chloe asked, as she got to her feet.

"I'm not sure," Jake said. "Why?"

"Because I have another lesson to add." She slid her arms around him. "*Lessons from Desiree* #40: 'Fairy tales really do come true.'"

Then she kissed her handsome Texas prince with all the love in her heart.

* * * * *

THE ROYAL HOUSE OF NIROLI
Always passionate, always proud.

The richest royal family in the world—united by
blood and passion, torn apart by deceit and desire.

Nestled in the azure blue of the Mediterranean Sea, the
majestic island of Niroli has prospered for centuries.
The Fierezza men have worn the crown with passion
and pride since ancient times. But now, as the king's
health declines, and his two sons have been tragically
killed, the crown is in jeopardy.

The clock is ticking—a new heir must be found before the king is forced to abdicate. By royal decree the
internationally scattered members of the Fierezza family are summoned to claim their destiny. But any person
who takes the throne must do so according to The Rules
of the Royal House of Niroli. Soon secrets and rivalries
emerge as the descendents of this ancient royal line vie
for position and power. Only a true Fierezza can become ruler—a person dedicated to their country, their
people…and their eternal love!

*Each month starting in July 2007,
Harlequin Presents is delighted to bring you
an exciting installment from*
THE ROYAL HOUSE OF NIROLI,
*in which you can follow the epic search
for the true Nirolian king.
Eight heirs, eight romances, eight fantastic stories!*

*Here's your chance to enjoy a sneak preview of the
first book delivered to you by royal decree….*

FIVE minutes later she was standing immobile in front of the study's window, her original purpose of coming in forgotten, as she stared in shocked horror at the envelope she was holding. Waves of heat followed by icy chills surged through her body. She could hardly see the address now through her blurred vision, but the crest on its left-hand front corner stood out, its *royal* crest, followed by the address: *HRH Prince Marco of Niroli....*

She didn't hear Marco's key in the apartment door, she didn't even hear him calling out her name. Her shock was so great that nothing could penetrate it. It encased her in a kind of bubble, which only concentrated the torment of what she was suffering and branded it on her brain so that it could never be forgotten. It was only finally pierced by the sudden opening of the study door as Marco walked in.

"Welcome home, *Your Highness*. I suppose I ought to curtsy." She waited, praying that he would laugh and tell her that she had got it all wrong, that the envelope she was holding, addressing him as Prince Marco of Niroli, was some silly mistake. But like a tiny candle flame shivering vulnerably in the dark, her hope trembled fearfully. And then the look in Marco's eyes extinguished it as cruelly as a hand placed callously over a dying person's face to stem their last breath.

"Give that to me," he demanded, taking the envelope from her.

"It's too late, Marco," Emily told him brokenly. "I know the truth now…" She dug her teeth in her lower lip to try to force back her own pain.

"You had no right to go through my desk," Marco shot back at her furiously, full of loathing at being caught off guard and forced into a position in which he was in the wrong, making him determined to find something he could accuse Emily of. "I trusted you…."

Emily could hardly believe what she was hearing. "No, you didn't trust me, Marco, and you didn't trust me because you knew that I couldn't trust you. And you knew that because you're a liar, and liars don't trust people because they know that they themselves cannot be trusted." She not only felt sick, she also felt as though she could hardly breathe. "You are Prince Marco of Niroli… How could you not tell me who you are and still live with me as intimately as we have lived together?" she demanded brokenly.

"Stop being so ridiculously dramatic," Marco

demanded fiercely. "You are making too much of the situation."

"*Too much?*" Emily almost screamed the words at him. "When were you going to tell me, Marco? Perhaps you just planned to walk away without telling me anything? After all, what do my feelings matter to you?"

"Of course they matter." Marco stopped her sharply. "And it was in part to protect them, and you, that I decided not to inform you when my grandfather first announced that he intended to step down from the throne and hand it over to me."

"To protect me?" Emily nearly choked on her fury. "Hand over the throne? No wonder you told me when you first took me to bed that all you wanted was sex. You *knew* that was the only kind of relationship there could ever be between us! You *knew* that one day you would be Niroli's king. No doubt you are expected to marry a princess. Is she picked out for you already, your *royal* bride?"

* * * * *

Look for
THE FUTURE KING'S PREGNANT MISTRESS
by Penny Jordan in July 2007,
from Harlequin Presents,
available wherever books are sold.

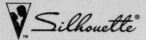

Romantic
SUSPENSE

**Sparked by Danger,
Fueled by Passion.**

Mission: Impassioned

A brand-new miniseries begins with

My Spy

By *USA TODAY* bestselling author

Marie Ferrarella

She had to trust him with her life....
It was the most daring mission of Joshua Lazlo's
career: rescuing the prime minister of England's
daughter from a gang of cold-blooded kidnappers.
But nothing prepared the shadowy secret agent
for a fiery woman whose touch ignited something
far more dangerous.

My Spy

#1472

Available July 2007 wherever you buy books!

Visit Silhouette Books at www.eHarlequin.com   SRS27542

Do you know
a real-life heroine?

Nominate her for the Harlequin More Than Words award.

Each year Harlequin Enterprises honors five
ordinary women for their extraordinary
commitment to their community.

Each recipient of the Harlequin More Than Words
award receives a $10,000 donation from Harlequin
to advance the work of her chosen charity. And five
of Harlequin's most acclaimed authors donate their
time and creative talents to writing a novella inspired
by the award recipients. The More Than Words
anthology is published annually in October and all
proceeds benefit causes of concern to women.

HARLEQUIN

More Than Words

**For more details or to nominate
a woman you know please visit**

www.HarlequinMoreThanWords.com

MTW2007

HARLEQUIN®

Blaze™

What would you do if you hit the jackpot?

Mild-mannered makeup artist Jane Kurtz gets everything she's ever wanted when she wins the lottery. Including the hot, sexy guy! But can it last?

SHE DID A BAD, BAD THING

by

STEPHANIE BOND

Don't miss the first book of Blaze's newest six-book continuity series...
MILLION DOLLAR SECRETS.

Available in July
wherever Harlequin books are sold.

www.eHarlequin.com

HB79342

THE ROYAL HOUSE OF NIROLI

Always passionate, always proud.

**The richest royal family in the world—
a family united by blood and passion,
torn apart by deceit and desire.**

Step into the glamorous, enticing world of the
Nirolian Royal Family. As the king ails he must find an
heir…each month an exciting new installment follows
the epic search for the true Nirolian king. Eight heirs,
eight romances, eight fantastic stories!

It's time for playboy prince Marco Fierezza to
claim his rightful place…on the throne of Niroli!
Emily loves Marco, but she has no idea he's a royal
prince! What will this king-in-waiting do when he
discovers his mistress is pregnant?

THE FUTURE KING'S PREGNANT MISTRESS

by Penny Jordan

(#2643)

On sale July 2007.

www.eHarlequin.com

HP12643

REQUEST YOUR FREE BOOKS!
2 FREE NOVELS PLUS 2 FREE GIFTS!

SPECIAL EDITION®
Life, Love and Family!

YES! Please send me 2 FREE Silhouette Special Edition® novels and my 2 FREE gifts. After receiving them, if I don't wish to receive any more books, I can return the shipping statement marked "cancel." If I don't cancel, I will receive 6 brand-new novels every month and be billed just $4.24 per book in the U.S., or $4.99 per book in Canada, plus 25¢ shipping and handling per book and applicable taxes, if any*. That's a savings of at least 15% off the cover price! I understand that accepting the 2 free books and gifts places me under no obligation to buy anything. I can always return a shipment and cancel at any time. Even if I never buy another book from Silhouette, the two free books and gifts are mine to keep forever.   235 SDN EEYU 335 SDN EEY6

Name	(PLEASE PRINT)	
Address		Apt.
City	State/Prov.	Zip/Postal Code

Signature (if under 18, a parent or guardian must sign)

Mail to the **Silhouette Reader Service™**:
IN U.S.A.: P.O. Box 1867, Buffalo, NY 14240-1867
IN CANADA: P.O. Box 609, Fort Erie, Ontario L2A 5X3
Not valid to current Silhouette Special Edition subscribers.

Want to try two free books from another line?
Call 1-800-873-8635 or visit www.morefreebooks.com.

* Terms and prices subject to change without notice. NY residents add applicable sales tax. Canadian residents will be charged applicable provincial taxes and GST. This offer is limited to one order per household. All orders subject to approval. Credit or debit balances in a customer's account(s) may be offset by any other outstanding balance owed by or to the customer. Please allow 4 to 6 weeks for delivery.

Your Privacy: Silhouette is committed to protecting your privacy. Our Privacy Policy is available online at www.eHarlequin.com or upon request from the Reader Service. From time to time we make our lists of customers available to reputable firms who may have a product or service of interest to you. If you would prefer we not share your name and address, please check here. ☐

SSE07

SPECIAL EDITION™

**Look for six new
MONTANA MAVERICKS
stories, beginning in July with**

THE MAN WHO HAD EVERYTHING

by CHRISTINE RIMMER

When Grant Clifton decided to sell the
family ranch, he knew it would devastate
Stephanie Julen, the caretaker who'd always been
like a little sister to him. He wanted a new start,
but how could he tell her that she and her mother
would have to leave...especially now that he was
head over heels in love with her?

MONTANA MAVERICKS

Dreaming big—and winning hearts—in Big Sky Country

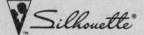

COMING NEXT MONTH

#1837 THE MAN WHO HAD EVERYTHING—
Christine Rimmer

Montana Mavericks: Striking It Rich

When Grant Clifton decided to sell the family ranch, how would he tell Stephanie Julen, the caretaker who'd always been like a little sister to him, that she and her mother would have to leave…especially now that he was head-over-heels in love with her? Was the man who had everything about to lose it all in a betrayal of the woman he was falling for?

#1838 THE PLAYBOY TAKES A WIFE—Crystal Green

As the new CEO of his family's corporation, scandal-sheet regular Lucas Chandler needed an image makeover fast. Visiting a Mexican orphanage seemed like the perfect PR ploy for the playboy—until volunteer and ultimate good girl Alicia Sanchez taught him a lesson in living the good life through good works…and lasting love.

#1839 A BARGAIN CALLED MARRIAGE—Kate Welsh

Her mother's troubled relationships had always cast a pall over Samantha Hopewell's own hunt for Mr. Perfect. Then Italian race-boat driver Niccolo Verdini came to recover from an accident at her family manor, and the healing began…in Samantha's heart.

#1840 HIS BROTHER'S GIFT—Mary J. Forbes

Alaskan bush pilot Will Rubens had carved out a carefree life for himself—until Savanna Stowe showed up on his doorstep with Will's orphaned nephew in tow. Will now found himself the guardian of a young autistic boy…but it was earth mother Savanna who quickly took custody of Will's affections.

#1841 THE RANCHER'S SECOND CHANCE—Nicole Foster

As childhood sweethearts, dirt-poor Rafe Garrett and wealthy Julene Santiago had let their differences tear them apart. Now, years later, Julene returned to town to help her ailing father—and ran smack dab into Rafe. Would the old, unbridgeable gulf reopen between them… or would the love of a lifetime get a second chance?

#1842 THE BABY BIND—Nikki Benjamin

After several unsuccessful attempts at conceiving left her marriage in tatters, Charlotte Fagan had one last hope—to adopt a foreign child. For the application to be approved, though, she and her estranged husband, Sean, would have to pretend to still be together. He agreed to go along with the plan—on one condition….

SSECNM0607